THE BODY IN BRANDEN BAY

KELLY MASON

LITTLE ORCHARD PRESS

Editor: Alison Knight

Cover Design by www.getcovers.com

This book was written in the UK and edited in British English, where some spelling, grammar and word usage will be different to US English.

Created with Vellum

For Gary <3 xx

CHAPTER 1

I'm Becky James. I was a city-slicking millennial, living and working in the financial district of London until I inherited a huge Victorian house from my glamorous grandma, Constance. The house is set right on the sea front at Branden Bay, a traditional seaside resort in the south west of England. The bay consists of a yellow horseshoe of sand and sports a posh hotel at one end and a traditional funfair at the other, with a pier jutting out to the sea. A wooded hill backs the town with a castle overlooking the popular tourist spot.

When Grandma died, I put the house up for sale, having no intention of moving in. I had been living with my boyfriend, Marcus, in his Thameside apartment for the past three years. However, our relationship came to an abrupt end and as we worked for the same company, I decided it was time for a complete change. So I took Grandma's house off the market and moved to the other side of the country to start a new life.

Whilst I loved my home by the sea, it was more than a tad spooky and I soon discovered that I'd inherited more than just Grandma's house – I'd gained her so-called gift as a medium. But I was scared of ghosts and didn't want to see the dead. All I wanted to do was concentrate on the café I had opened in the large front room of the house. I decided I would ignore anything spooky and concentrate on building my café business. To this end, I visited the local bank for help.

"Take a seat, Miss James," said Mr Stone as he looked down his nose at my loan application. "So, you've opened a café on the seafront called." He paused and brought the page closer to his eyes as if he was short-sighted. "Connie's Café?"

"That's right and it's really successful," I said, the enthusiasm oozing from my voice. I shifted in my seat. I guess it was rare for someone in their mid-twenties to own such a large house on the seafront and run a café. "People love my cakes and I need a professional coffee machine to be able to meet growing demand."

"Hmm, as excited as you are over your recent success, I see you've only been open for – two weeks?" He stared at me and raised his eyebrows as if to say, *you silly girl.*

"Sixteen days, actually."

"And where did your initial investment come

from?" He flicked through the pages I had printed off to support my application.

"I inherited the house and a little money from my Grandmother."

"I see." He shook his head.

"I heard your bank supports small businesses." I pointed to the poster on the wall depicting a suited man handing over a decent-sized wedge of cash to a plumber. I gave him a friendly smile. I knew I'd come to the right place – their adverts were on TV every night.

He frowned. "Indeed. But run before you can walk comes to mind in this case."

"My poor percolator's working overtime. I can't keep up with the filtered coffee orders. It's essential that I invest in a commercial coffee machine to enable me to offer a wide variety of hot drinks, from espresso to latte, to meet the growing demand of my customer base." *Did that sound business-like?* I thought. I'd read a similar spiel in the blurb about the coffee machine online.

He turned the page. "You're not making any profits."

The guy was hard work. "It's a start up?" I sat up straight and stared him in the eye with what I hoped was an expression dazzling with confidence. When I'd worked in the City of London, I'd dealt with all sorts of people in the hard and fast world of the financial sector. Okay, so I mostly took their coats and poured coffee but still, I was sure I could schmooze this back-water bank manager – or *Assistant Manager,* as I read on his name badge.

I took a deep breath. "The takings are really good, as you can see from the projections I've provided. But my outgoings have been huge. Obvs – I've only just opened." *Whoops! Did I say that last bit out loud?* I thought.

"I fear your venture may have novelty value." He gave me a steely glare over the top of his glasses.

"Novelty? It's coffee and cake." I found it hard to keep the sarcasm from my voice and was two cat hairs away from telling him where to stick it.

Talking of cat hairs, I felt movement against my leg which was resting against one of my designer tote bags. Inside was Constance, the stray cat I'd taken in and named after Grandma. Constance followed me everywhere and she wriggled again. Worried she might pop out and cause a scene, I leaned down and gently stroked the top of her fluffy-topped ginger head hoping she would settle down.

I felt short bursts of air hit my face as Mr Stone flicked through the final pages of my cobbled-together business plan, far more quickly than he could possibly read it. I sighed. I knew what he was hinting at though, when he'd referred to the café having novelty value. I'd become the subject of local gossip since one of my new friends, Izzy, an ex- model and food critic who was in the process of elevating her career to full-time reporter, did an exclusive on me in the Gazette, hailing me as a paranormal detective after I'd solved a mystery concerning the disappearance of a local girl with the assistance of her father's shadowy ghost. It was something I was trying to distance myself from and forget. It was down to circumstance rather than any skill on my part that I located their bodies. And I nearly got myself killed in the process. Yes, I saw ghosts, but in no way was I a detective. I was brought back to the present by the sound of Mr Stone's voice.

"I see you have a personal overdraft."

"I'm within my limit."

"And two credit cards."

"Yes that's right." I pulled at the neckline of my top. I'd maxed out on credit buying supplies.

"Leave it with me and we'll review the matter and let you know," he said, pushing my business plan to one side.

I felt it was one of those 'don't-call-us-we'll-call-you' moments that I'd experienced many times when chasing parts in West End shows, armed with my performing arts degree.

"Thanks for your help," I said, picking up my tote bag. Constance poked her fluffy head out and hissed at Mr Stone. He took a sharp intake of breath and his brows knitted together. I quickly slipped out of the bank with my head down.

Once outside, I scolded the mound of ginger fluff in my bag, wagging my finger at her. "Constance, that won't have helped. I'll leave you locked up at home if you carry on like this."

I'd bought Constance a proper pet bag made from a durable material with a neat little window she could look out of. But my feline companion was just as much of a designer diva as her namesake. She'd sniffed her nose at it, sashayed away and got back into Grandma's designer tote bag. But I loved Constance the cat. She felt like family, what with her having the trademark red hair and green eyes which I also possessed.

Feeling someone's gaze upon me, I glanced across the street. I shivered as I saw a man staring at me from the opposite pavement. He had a neat beard and dark hair and wore a business suit. I squinted at him and his gaze caught mine. I felt a pang of sadness in my heart as he looked at me intently. I felt as if he was drawing me in with his stare. I pulled my eyes away. *He's probably someone who's seen the spread about me in the local rag*, I thought as I turned away. I pulled my sunglasses from the top of my head and walked along the sloping High Street towards the seafront. I felt a short burst of static in the nape of my neck and quickly rubbed it away. After a few steps, I glanced over my shoulder to check if the man was still there, but he was gone.

Constance popped her head out of the bag and meowed at me as if in sympathy.

I sighed. "It seems we're no closer to getting funds for one of those swanky, shiny coffee machines. We'll have to resort to selling instant at this rate." It was embarrassing. "What self-respecting café owner serves up coffee made from granules?"

Constance meowed as though she agreed.

As the promenade came into view, white crests covered the waves as they charged towards the shore. I pulled my coat tight as my skirt flapped against my legs. It was mid-June, and a warm one at that, but some days could be blustery with the unpredictable nature of British weather. As I turned onto Beach Road, which ran parallel to the Victorian-style prom, Constance jumped out of my bag and onto the wall, trotting along beside me with her coat ruffling in the wind.

I reached the large terraced Victorian house which had been my home now for a couple of months. The front door was painted a glossy blue. This remained my private entrance. A large bay housed a floor to ceiling window with French doors, which were currently wide open. This was the café entrance. The sign above the door had 'Connie's Café' written on it and a picture of a fluffy ginger puss, just like Constance the cat.

As I entered the café, the hubbub from customers warmed my heart. About half of the tables were filled. Annie, one of my newly-found friends, looked up and I smiled. She was on a week's holiday from work and for some unknown reason had chosen to spend it working with me. She grinned back, her blonde-tinged brown afro matched her brown and gold print dress. She looked as sunny on the outside as she was on the inside. Annie always had a calming influence on me.

"Sorry I'm late back," I said, taking off my jacket and putting on my floral apron. "Business is booming, eh?"

Annie nodded. "I've had a constant stream of customers."

I joined her behind the makeshift counter, which was in fact a table I'd borrowed from a neighbour. "Don't get too excited. I'm not feeling confident after the trip to the bank."

"Did they give you a hard time?" she asked with her eyebrows raised and a hand on her hip.

"The way he treated me, I felt silly for asking. But he said he'd let me know." I looked towards the entrance as Mrs Jessup from next door walked in. I called out to her. "Take any seat." At least the customers believed in me and were prepared to come in, sit at a hotchpotch of tables and pay cash-only.

"Well, I'm sure the bank will lend you the money. This place is amazing. Everyone's talking about it." Annie was a real cheerleader but I didn't have quite as much confidence as she did after the meeting with Mr Stone.

"Thanks for your help, Annie, I really appreciate it.'

"I wish I could work here instead of the pier."

"Why?"

"Things are tense over there. We had the insurance agent in today – accidents are happening all over the place. Someone is suing them because a tile fell on their head. I might be out of a job at this rate."

"Oh no. As soon as I turn a profit, I'll give you some money to pay for the hours you've done here."

Annie laughed. "No need – I love helping out. The atmosphere is amazing. Honestly it's fun."

I smiled. Annie was a good tonic. I felt the tension I'd picked up in the bank ebb away.

Annie opened her soft brown eyes and swallowed. "Someone was here looking for you earlier." She turned away to wipe the table top down with a cloth.

"Oh yes?" I said, picking up my pencil and pad. Mrs Jessup looked ready to order.

"A Mia Hart," Annie said. "She spoke to you last week?"

I remembered the name. "Was it about a cake order?"

Annie looked away scrubbing at the table. "No. It was about your paranormal investigation business." She turned, giving me a guilty smile.

"You know that's not a thing, right?" I placed a hand on my hip. "I hope you told her I can't help with anything paranormal?" So many people had been leaving me their details about ghosts and solving mysteries. Although it wasn't a complete negative as most of them stayed for tea and cake once they'd feasted their eyes on my bakes.

"Mia said she'd already spoken to you. She wants

someone to investigate the murder of her husband, Robert. You know, the body in the bay?"

I felt a tingle down my neck. A picture flashed in my mind of a patch on the beach which had been cordoned off with police tape. And a smartly-dressed blonde woman who had approached me on the café opening day. "Oh yes, I remember." She'd asked me to help her discover what happened to her husband who had been found washed up on the shore. "I told her already. I can't help. And I thought the Gazette reported yesterday that the coroner ruled it was suicide?"

"Seems his wife disagrees. Poor thing. I know you're not interested in your gift but she was desperate to speak to you. I didn't have the heart to send her away."

I put my hand to the back of my neck as I felt a shot of static. *I'm not going down that route again,* I thought. "I can't help her – remember? I'm not a psychic detective. That was fake news."

I gave a short but nervous laugh as I walked towards Mrs Jessup who was waving at me over her menu. I called over my shoulder to Annie. "I just want to concentrate on baking."

After taking Mrs Jessup's order, which was a pot of tea and a slice of cherry layer cake, I went through to the kitchen where Annie was already boiling the kettle.

"Mia is desperate to see you," she said.

"But I'm no detective. And there's no missing body

in this case. We know where it is. The newspaper said it's been released to the undertakers. I understand the memorial service is planned for next week."

"True, but I felt awful for her. So I said you'd call back, to let her know." Annie handed me an order slip, upon which she'd scribbled Mia's number.

I shook my head. "I'll call her this evening. But it's definitely no." I placed the paper in the pocket of my apron and glanced at the clock. It was twelve already and the lunch time rush would start soon.

I took a filled pot of tea out of the kitchen and into the main café. After placing it on Mrs Jessup's table, I fetched her cake.

The sea breeze blew my hair as I rearranged chairs around the café tables on the front patio, in case any customers wanted to brave a blustery alfresco lunch. Constance perched herself on the wall touting for strokes from passers-by. She hissed and I looked up as static shot up my back. The suited guy I'd seen earlier in the High Street was across the road, leaning against the sea wall of the prom.

CHAPTER 2

It was the lunch time rush at the café. I'd filled my last table when I heard a familiar voice.

"Hi lovey." It was Lynn. She ran a spiritualist church, in a hut which backed onto my garden. It was she who had loaned me a few tables and chairs for the café, which were seeing me through until I got my business off the ground. While I liked Lynn and knew she meant well, she was forever encouraging me to explore my 'gift' – as she called it. I considered the ability to see the dead to be more of a curse and the last thing I wanted was to encourage any more paranormal activity.

"I thought I'd pop by and see how you're getting on," Lynn said nodding towards the room full of customers. "By the looks of it, you're doing a marvellous job."

"Come on in, I've got orders to take. I'll get you a tea."

Rather than taking a seat, Lynn helped Annie and myself serve. After taking orders, I refilled the percolator in the kitchen and turned to Lynn, who had followed me in. "I'm trying to raise funds for a commercial coffee machine because I'm fighting to keep up with demand."

Annie came to the door. "Three more coffees and two sandwich platters."

"Your takings must be amazing," said Lynn. "I'll stay until the rush is over. I've not got to be back yet."

"Thanks," I said turning around to grab a couple of pre-prepared sandwich platters. "I need to invest in this place though. I went to the bank this morning with a loan request, but I didn't get the feeling it went that well."

"Hang on in there, lovey, and have faith," she said. "It'll be the school holidays at the end of next month and you're bound to have a steady stream of customers. You'll save up in no time for that coffee machine you're after, I'm sure."

"I do hope so."

"You're doing a super job, Becky."

"I wish Mr Stone at the bank could see that."

At two p.m, Lynn removed her apron. "I'd better get back now. Good luck, girls and if you need any more help, let me know."

. . .

At four o'clock I closed up, having waved Annie off. Static shot up my back and I jumped. I noticed the man in the pin-striped suit again, over at the prom. *Who is that guy?* I thought and was just about to turn away, when a woman walked up the path. She was blonde and wore an emerald shift dress with a snazzy handbag over the crook of her arm. I vaguely recognised her then realised it was Mia Hart.

She smiled at me as I reopened the door. "Your assistant said you'd call me back?"

"I've been rushed off my feet today. I was just about to contact you to say ..."

Mia squeezed past me into the café. "I'm hoping that you can help me, because I'm quite desperate." She snapped open her Ted Baker handbag. Pulling out a fancy hankie, she dabbed at her eyes as she blinked her fake-eyelash-adorned lids.

My shoulders drooped as I closed the café door. "I'll make tea." I wished I'd called her earlier to let her know I could be of no help.

Five minutes later, I sat with Mia drinking tea as we ate the last slices of that day's Victoria sponge. It was dusted with icing sugar and had a buttercream filling, just like Grandma used to make.

Mia nodded as she swallowed a mouthful of cake and took a sip of her tea before looking deep into my eyes. "As you know, I don't believe it was suicide that resulted in Rob being washed up on the beach."

"Why do you think it wasn't suicide?"

"He would never do that. Rob hated water – he couldn't even swim."

"But if he wanted to kill himself? Wouldn't that be a bonus?"

Mia frowned and I regretted my choice of words but it had been a long day. My head was banging and after all, I wasn't out to impress her – I was actually trying to impress upon her that I wasn't the answer to her problem.

Her bottom lip trembled. "I'm sure he would have gone for something far quicker."

"Why do the police think it was suicide?"

"They found a note on his desk at work."

Definitely suicide then, I thought. The poor woman clearly could not accept the truth. I felt sorry for her though. Must be absolutely awful.

"I told them it was obviously a fake suicide note. I asked to be sent the letter, to check that it was his handwriting. But whenever I've called, they've fobbed me off."

"If you think someone faked a suicide note – are you saying he was killed?" I gulped. I certainly didn't want to get mixed up in a murder investigation.

"I guess so, although I don't know people around town myself. Robert spent weekdays in Branden Bay and only came home to Devon on the odd weekend. He was ever so busy with his work."

"Did he have a property in town, then?"

"No. He had an account at the Budget Inn."

"If the police are convinced it's suicide, how do you think I can help?"

"As you're a psychic detective, I presumed that you'd tune in to his spirit and find out."

I needed to nip this in the bud. I took a deep breath. "I don't call people up. Spirits only contact me if they need help." I thumbed over my shoulder. "But you could go to the spiritualist church in Castle Road. It's situated in an old scout hut which backs onto my garden." I smiled. "Ask for Lynn. She's really lovely and I'm sure she could help."

"No, I like you. I feel I can trust you."

I sighed inwardly. I thought I'd made it clear I didn't have the right skills.

Mia dabbed her eyes with her hankie. "Robert's life insurance policy doesn't cover suicide. I'll have to sell my home, it's mortgaged. What will become of me?"

As the coroner had ruled that Robert killed himself, Mia was going to be left in financial hardship. In my opinion, that was enough to severely impair her judgement.

Mia hiccupped. "I haven't worked in years."

"I see." There was no way I wanted to get tangled up in that sort of mess. I guessed Mia was in her late thirties. Maybe forties if she'd had a little help from a cosmetic doctor and was clearly used to living on easy street. My sympathy began to ebb, especially if her motivation was financial. How on earth could I prove he was murdered when quite frankly – it was plain to see – the guy had killed himself.

"Rob was in a high-paid job. A director of Chesham Financial Services," said Mia. "But I'll have nothing, unless you can prove it wasn't suicide. If Rob didn't kill himself, then I'll get a large pay-out from the life insurance. Out of that I can make a sizeable payment to you. About six thousand?"

Six thousand? Wow, I thought, nearly choking on the last of my cake. That'd cover the coffee machine, a year's supply of beans and a few months' worth of take-out cups. I had a fleeting moment of weakness but soon came to my senses. The guy had clearly killed himself – so I couldn't help.

"Your lovely assistant Annie was telling me how you'd gone to the bank for a loan?"

Did she now? I thought as a faint buzz moved up the back of my neck. I rubbed it away. "Look, I sympathise with your position, but the article written about my paranormal detecting in the Gazette was exaggerated."

"There's no need to be so modest." She stood up. "Promise me you'll at least think about it?"

No, I thought, but still nodded.

"I'll call you tomorrow." She hung her bag over her arm and walked towards the door.

I baked in a frenzy that evening, wondering how I was going to fob Mia off.

As I got into my night clothes, Constance sat on the windowsill, looking out to the prom and hissed. I pulled the curtains and she jumped onto the bed, pawing at the duvet until she decided it was comfortable enough to settle on. I felt a buzz of static and rubbed my neck, pushing thoughts of Mia out of my mind. I wished people would leave me alone with their paranormal requests, I didn't want to experience contact from sprits ever again.

A couple of days of bad weather passed, it wasn't great for business but at least I managed to get on top of my supplies and made a batch of sponges for the freezer. I'd watched out for any response from Mr Stone. I'd received a couple of letters, but none were from the bank. I needed to set time aside for paperwork and crunch numbers. I wondered whether Mr Stone had been right, that I had indeed run before I could walk. With zilch-o experience of running a business, self-doubt slopped all over me like a thick custard on a jam pudding.

The morning sunshine beamed in as I sat in my snug, eating a bowl of cereal as the sun shone through the French doors. I'd decided to open up at half ten, to give myself a thirty minute break before I started. The snug was what I called my private lounge at the back of the house, which looked out onto my rear back garden, consisting of a lush green lawn surrounded by evergreen bushes and an apple tree to one side with a bench underneath, where Grandma used to sit. I knew this glorious day would be great for business and that I'd be rushed off my feet now that Annie was back working on the pier. I'd managed to assemble the cakes in good time, so decided to have a relaxing half hour before I opened. Constance rubbed against my legs and I picked her up.

"Do you want salmon for breakfast?" She purred at me as I hugged her close. I carried her into the kitchen.

Constance licked her lips after finishing her fishy breakfast and sashayed out of the kitchen, no doubt to curl up on my sofa in the snug.

I checked my smart phone as I ate a slice of toast made with a homemade loaf. I hadn't quite mastered the art of baking bread and it would be some time before I felt confident to serve up my own, but I was getting there. It was a seeded loaf and maybe the texture was not perfect and there were way too many air holes, but it tasted delish. A notification pinged on my phone screen, it was from the bank alerting me to a secure communication.

My heart thumped as I logged into my mobile banking app and brought up the message.

We are sorry to inform you that your loan application has been declined at this time.

I put my phone on the table mumbling a strong word under my breath. I heard knocking from the cafe. *Who's that? We don't open yet,* I thought, hoping it was a delivery.

My heart dropped when I reached the cafe and saw

Mia Hart tapping on the window. I opened the door for her.

"Hello Becky," Mia said. "I know you're probably still thinking about it, but I've just picked up some personal effects from Rob's office and I had to speak to someone." She hiccupped.

"Right," I said, hoping the disappointment did not show on my face.

"Regardless of whether you take the case on or not – I really need a friendly face." She burst into tears.

Oh dear – there goes my thirty minutes of relaxation, I thought. "Come inside," I said, opening the door wide and stepping to one side to allow her to walk in. She held a carrier bag in her hand from a budget clothes store.

I shut the door.

Mia followed me towards the kitchen. "It was awful, I lost my temper at the Chesham offices."

"I'll put the kettle on. I've got some lovely breakfast tea in."

Mia wiped her eyes and I noticed one of her fake eyelashes had partly detached itself. "I shouted at that madam of a receptionist and lost it. I told her I knew my Robert had been murdered and I was going to find out who did it, come what may."

"Surely they understand you're grieving?" I said, imagining the scene she must have caused.

She shook her head. "The receptionist called security and the guard led me outside." She lifted up the carrier. "Then the senior partner, Graham, came out and passed me this." She turned her nose up at the store logo on the bag. "He told me it was probably best if I didn't visit the offices again." She shook her head. "After everything Rob did for that firm." Her crying turned into a deep sob.

"I'll take you into my snug," I said, hoping the view of the garden would calm her down.

"Please help me, Becky. Everyone thinks I'm mad but I'm convinced he was murdered. I'll give you two thousand now and if you prove it wasn't suicide, I'll give you another four. If you're unsuccessful then fine, just keep the two thousand – at least I'll know in my heart that I tried."

I swallowed. I really needed money to pay my credit card bill, but there was no way I could take it under false pretences. After all, I had no idea how to call up her dead husband.

Mia sat down and opened the carrier bag. "I'll show you what they gave me from his office. Maybe you can get a feel for his spirit through these items?"

I took a deep breath and sat beside her. I didn't want to invite any attention from dead people, not after last time. Still, she was upset and I felt I should at least look interested.

The first thing she took out of the bag was a set of keys. "Can you feel anything spiritual?" she said as she held them up.

I took them from her.

"I've no idea what they're for," she said.

They looked as if they were keys to a large house, or an apartment building, because they had a fob attached, the sort that opened electric gates. Holding the keys in my hand, I could not feel anything spiritual, indeed I never expected to, but her gaze was so intense I felt under pressure. "Hmm, maybe?" I put the keys on the coffee table.

She placed the other items next to the keys. A small desk clock, a pen set, a pair of tickets to see *Mamma Mia* at the Bristol Hippodrome and finally she passed me a photo frame. "This is Robert standing with Graham when the firm had won an award." She wiped her eyes again. "Robert admired that man so much and all he's done is chuck his stuff in a carrier from a tacky shop." Tears tumbled down her cheeks. "Carrying that bag out of the offices was so humiliating."

I took the photo. "What?" I meant to say to myself, but it came out loud.

Mia stared at me. "Are you getting something?"

Static shot up my back. My mouth went dry and I felt dizzy. Staring back at me was Robert Hart, wearing a suit, with dark hair and a neatly trimmed beard.

Constance appeared at the door with her back arched and her hair sticking up on end.

"Is something coming through?" Mia grabbed my forearm; her eyes opened wide and her fake eyelash had migrated down her cheek.

I rubbed away the static, now accompanied by

chills covering my entire body like a wave of surf up the beach. A vision of the suited guy who I'd seen outside the bank, and on the prom appeared in my mind – he'd seemed so real. But looking at this picture now, he was clearly Robert's ghost.

I stood up. "I'll pour the tea," I said. "Then we'll go through everything."

Some minutes later, as I held my tea cup, I heard it rattle on the saucer. Constance gave a low meow. I was about to take a path I hoped I would not regret. I feared Robert's ghost would stalk me until I found his killer. I had no other choice. I had to accept Mia's cry for help.

CHAPTER 3

It proved to be a busy day and especially hard work for me as Annie was back working on the pier. I could not fall into bed for an early night, as I was expecting visitors. Early evening arrived and I removed a roasted chicken from the oven and placed it on the worktop. Constance watched, swishing her tail in anticipation of a treat. I heard a rap at the back door. It was Lynn. There was a gate at the end of my garden, which led to the spiritualist hut and she often used that route rather than walking around the block.

"Come in," I said as I opened the door.

"Hope you don't mind me showing up unannounced, lovey. Ooh, expecting guests?"

"I'm making dinner for Annie, Izzy and H." Izzy and H had been friends with Annie for years and they met up once a month in each other's houses for a meal.

Since I had joined the friendship group, it was my turn.

"Oh yes?"Lynn grinned and raised her eyebrows "H?"

I shook my head. The whole of Branden Bay seemed to think that I was having some sort of romance with the local police detective, known to his friends as 'H'. But he was not my type. I didn't go for obviously good-looking, muscle-rippling guys. And I was sure he didn't find me attractive either – he was forever criticising me.

Lynn bent down to pet Constance.

"I'm glad you came in. It's happened again," I said.

"What – H asked you out?" Lynn looked up.

"No." I frowned at her, was Lynn trying to match-make? "I've had contact."

"You've had a sighting? Of a spirit?" She returned to standing.

"Yes, but it's not like last time. It wasn't a shadow or a see-through projection." I shuddered. "I thought he was a real person – flesh and blood."

"That'll be your gift developing, lovey." Lynn put a hand to her chest and looked excited as if her child had just taken her first steps. "Spirits come in many forms. It's not a physical world, what you see is your mind trying to interpret what your third eye is perceiving."

I shook my head. "I don't want a third eye. I'm perfectly happy with two."

"It's a process, lovey. I do wish you'd let me help. Who is it?"

"Robert Hart."

Lynn's eyes widened. "The body in the bay?"

"Yes. His wife, Mia, wants me to investigate. She thinks he would never have killed himself."

"If he's in your sights there must be a wrong that needs to be righted. Are you going to take it on?" Lynn took a seat at the table and Constance settled herself on her lap.

"She's paid me two thousand up front. It hit my bank account an hour ago."

"Marvellous. How can I help? Do you want me to arrange a seance?"

I shook my head and wrung my hands. "No thanks." Lynn didn't seem to grasp the fact that I was petrified of such things. "Mia's given me some background information I can start work on."

"Like what?"

I filled the kettle. "He graduated from Exeter University, and joined Chesham Financial Services as a trainee at their Devon office, eventually becoming a director at the age of thirty-five and transferring to the Branden Bay branch." I flicked the kettle to boil and turned to face Lynn. "He liked to holiday in Italy. It's strange, but she had only sketchy details of his day-to-day life in Branden Bay. They'd only been seeing each other at the weekends, when he returned to their main house in Devon." I took a couple of cups out of the cupboard. "She didn't say it, but I'm guessing the marriage was on the rocks."

"Nice that she still loves him enough to care about looking into a possible murder," said Lynn.

"Well, she won't get her insurance pay-out if it was suicide."

"I see. If the marriage was in trouble you might not be able to trust her. I don't want you getting into any danger. It will be much easier if you just let me help you, lovey – rather than discover the truth the hard way and getting yourself into hot water. Look what happened last time."

"I'll let you know if I need help. Tell me what you've been up to, Lynn."

I listened as she talked about a trip to Bristol she'd taken to see her sister, as we finished off our tea.

The doorbell rang and Lynn stood up. "I don't want to intrude but make sure you ask for help developing your gift. It's your time."

I nodded at her but thought, *no thank you.*

Lynn left by the back door and I went to the front with Constance sashaying ahead.

"Come through," I said to Annie as I opened the door.

She followed me to the kitchen. "The food smells amazing."

"I've decided to keep things simple and cook a traditional family meal. With dinner times usually only including me and the cat, I don't often cook a full roast and it's a good excuse to add all the trimmings."

"So did you speak to that Mia Hart?"

"Yes, she popped by this morning."

"How did she react when you said you couldn't help her?"

"Well ..." I felt the heat rush to my cheeks.

"You didn't?"

I nodded. "I took it on." I told Annie about Mia's visit in detail as we drank wine.

"Do you think he was murdered then?"

"If he wasn't – I doubt he'd be following me around." I put the veg on to steam and the doorbell rang again.

I found both Izzy and H on the threshold.

"Darling," said Izzy as she gave me a double air kiss. "I've been so looking forward to this." She glided in like a tall swan with her perfect blonde bob.

"Don't expect too much," I said. "It's only home-style food and my cooking isn't on the same level as my baking."

"Don't put yourself down, sweetie. I'm sure it's going to be amazing."

"Alright?" said H. "Long time no see."

I felt the heat rise to my cheeks and I stepped aside. I didn't want to embrace him. As much as I appreciated that H was a nice person, he'd even saved my life, there was something about him that unnerved me, something that got under my skin. As per usual, he was looking so obviously chiselled, with his bulging muscles visible through his black t-shirt and in blue jeans which fit ... snugly. Detective Blake looked more like a body-builder than a copper.

"How's it going?" I asked moving my hair out of my eyes.

"I passed my sergeant's exam and training starts on the first of the month."

"Next week?"

"Yep, I'll be in Bristol for training."

"Better not let the local villains know that," I said. "They'll be up to no good."

H laughed. "I'm sure the local force will cope without me."

AFTER OUR MEAL OF CHICKEN WITH ROASTED PARSNIPS, potatoes, peas, carrots and broccoli doused in a thick gravy, we all sat back in our seats. Constance finished off a saucer of chicken I had put down for her. I'd bought a cat bowl but she would not eat out of it? Nope – it had to be dished up on Grandma's Royal Doulton dinner service.

"I'm absolutely stuffed," said Annie after we'd finished eating. "That was totally yummy."

"I agree, darling. It was a hug on a plate," said Izzy.

"Certainly hit the spot for me," said H, picking up his bottle of beer and taking a slug.

"As you're out of town," Annie said to H, "who's going to be investigating the murder of Robert Hart?"

H frowned. "Murder? That was suicide."

"That's not what Becky heard," she said nodding at me.

I stared into my drink, feeling H's gaze on my cheeks as if his eyes were lasers.

"What are you up to now?" he said in a stern voice, placing his empty bottle on the table.

I felt heat rise up my neck. "Nothing. I just had a visit from his wife, that's all."

"Don't get involved. Concentrate on your cakes."

Constance jumped onto H's lap and purred as he rubbed her neck.

I crossed my arms. "His wife doesn't seem to think it was suicide and to be honest neither do I."

"How would you know?" H gave a short laugh.

I couldn't say it was because I'd seen the dead Robert wandering about town. H wasn't a lover of the spiritual side of things and it would make me look a little weird. "She said he hated water." Was all I could think to say.

H shook his head and sighed. "Great evidence."

I clenched my teeth to prevent myself from saying something rude.

Izzy watched intently. "So you've got a new case?"

There wasn't much point in lying. "Yes I have," I said and gave H a smirk.

H sat back and Constance purred as he scratched

her head. "You're wasting your time; she's already complained to us for not investigating it. We've got a suicide note and sent it off to the graphologist with a sample of his handwriting from the office."

"It'll be interesting to see what their response is, won't it?" I said picking up my wine glass as if I already knew it would come back as a forgery.

"We got it back today, they confirmed that the suicide note was definitely signed by Robert Hart."

"Maybe they made a mistake?" I said.

"They're pretty accurate. It came back as a 99.9 percent match. And why would he write a suicide note if he wasn't planning to top himself?"

"I guess that's what I need to find out. Isn't it?" I smiled sweetly.

H's pupils dilated until his eyes looked black. I glanced away as I felt the heat pricking my face. H had a point though, a suicide note signed by the victim wasn't a good indication of murder.

I placed my wine glass back on the table. "Maybe he was tortured and forced to write it."

"I think the post mortem would have flagged up any signs of thumb screws."

"What did the post mortem show?"

"Leave it to the big boys, Becky."

He's pushing it now, I thought as I crossed my arms.

"Come on you two," said Annie probably sensing the tension.

"Cool it with the tiff, my darlings," added Izzy. "Either make up, or get a room."

I blushed hard, why on earth did they think we fancied each other? It was beyond me.

H had a smug look on his face. "If anyone killed him, it was his crazy wife. We had a complaint come in. She went psycho over at Chesham's offices. They want to take out a court order to keep her away."

"Mia seems perfectly respectable to me." I uncrossed my arms.

H laughed. "I don't think your judgement of character is always spot on."

I narrowed my eyes. "Well, Detective Sergeant Blake, if you're so confident he committed suicide, you won't have to worry about me falling into the clutches of a murderer. So I've nothing to worry about, have I?"

Izzy pulled a notepad out of her bag and scribbled away at the page.

"What are you doing?" I asked. "You're not critiquing my home roast for the Gazette's culinary column, are you?"

She shook her head. "If this is going to turn into a big story, I need to collect the facts from the off."

H laughed. "It won't be turning into anything at all. It's just a sad woman trying to get an insurance claim approved."

Izzy arched one of her eyebrows. "My job is going to be on the line if I don't come up with another good story. I'll be put on obituaries, or worse, covering the upcoming season of school summer fairs." She gave a delicate groan.

"So you're giving me a deadline?" I asked Izzy.

"Well, it would be super cool If you could wrap it up in a couple of weeks, darling."

To be honest, that deadline suited me, too. The two thousand up front helped with my bills but I'd need the balancing payment of four thousand if I had any hope of buying that new coffee machine.

Annie laughed. "What are you all like? Are we going to play cards? Or have a boxing match? Come on, I feel like thrashing you all at poker."

I fetched the cards and poker chips from the sideboard, made coffee and let my guests sample the new chocolate-covered flapjacks I'd made. They were divine. The buttery oats and chocolate coating soothed my annoyance with H. We polished off the whole batch and the atmosphere changed as we played cards. Annie indeed ended up beating us all.

CHAPTER 4

I shuddered as I climbed the stairs to bed. I felt as if someone was following me up. But as I swung around, only Constance was there. After I'd washed and pulled on my nightdress, I eased into the bed and pulled the covers up. Constance made herself comfortable beside me and I drifted off to a sleep, which was peppered with dreams of the café, of my friends, of my family – but in the background there was always Robert, staring at me from the distance.

I woke as I heard the grandfather clock strike two from the hall. Apart from the chimes reverberating through the house, it was silent.

Static shot up my spine. "Oh no," I said as I turned over and clutched the spare pillow. I kept my eyes shut, not wanting to find a spirit lurking in my room.

Constance gave a low wail and I felt her jump from the bed.

"Not now." I turned my head. I snapped my eyes open. There was no sign of a ghost. I scanned the room and took a deep breath to try and slow the thump of my heartbeat.

Constance sat on the windowsill and hissed.

Pins and needles filled my hands as I pushed myself up in the bed. I threw the covers off, stood up and crept over to the curtains. I pulled them back and gulped as I looked out to the prom. Leaning against the seawall, something was glowing. It was Robert.

Constance pawed at the pane.

I lifted the sash to get a better look, maybe he wasn't there and I was still dreaming.

Constance climbed onto the ledge.

"Get back inside." I leaned out to grab her.

Then she was gone, flying down from the windowsill.

"Connie," I shouted, into the quiet night where the only other noise was the gentle swishing sound from a calm sea. I leaned over, my heart beating fast, to see she'd landed on the table below.

Constance looked up and meowed.

"Stay there," I called.

She ignored me and jumped from the table towards my front wall.

"Oh for goodness sake," I said as I closed the window.

Pulling my robe from the back of the bedroom door, I put it on.

“That cat’s going to be the death of me,” I said as I ran down the stairs in my slippers. I grabbed my keys from the hall table and opened the front door.

Once on the threshold, I saw Robert glowing from the other side of the road. He turned and moved along the prom towards town. I heaved a sigh of relief. “Come inside,” I said in a loud whisper to my cat who was still perched on the wall, staring after Robert. She Jumped to the path and sashayed away in Robert’s direction.

“Get back here!” I stepped out of the house in my fluffy footwear, pulling the robe around me. When I reached the pavement, Constance was already about five yards away. I huffed and padded back to the front door pulling it shut, then returned to the pavement. Connie was following Robert’s ghost which was now on our side of the road, glowing about ten feet in front of her.

My knees prickled with static and I stopped to take in a few deep breaths, then broke into a jog. Going as fast as my slippers allowed.

Constance waited for me at the foot of the High Street. As I reached her, I stretched my arms out to grab her. She hissed and dodged me as static fuzzed in my hands. Robert’s ghost continued up the High Street. A sharp burst of static zapped my neck. I hesitated but he stopped and caught my gaze as a feeling of loss thumped into my chest to the point where I felt a lump form in my throat. I realised I had to push fear to one side, I'd already been given two thousand pounds to solve his murder.

Constance trotted up the empty High Street in pursuit of Robert and I followed, until he turned down Alma Road, which led to the town's only office block. As I rounded the corner, the modern glass-fronted offices came into view, glinting in the streetlamps. They were sandwiched between Victorian buildings and while it was not an ugly structure, it looked out of place. The offices were home to a few firms, one of which was Chesham Financial Services. I continued towards the building, where Robert approached the locked revolving doors and floated inside.

Constance meowed at the window. I noted from a plaque outside, that Chesham Financial Services, were situated on the second floor. Inside the lobby, there was a desk with a computer screen lighting up a security guard's face as he sat before it. The guard was oblivious to the ghostly visitor. Robert reached the lift door and stared back at me. My knees trembled as intense electricity buzzed through my body. I lifted my hand to my throat. The security guard looked up.

"He's seen us," I said to Constance as she pawed at the window.

I gave the guard a small wave then reached out and grabbed my cat who wriggled in my arms.

The guard exited the building and approached me. "Can I help you miss?"

"My cat ran off."

"You shouldn't come out alone at night." He was about my dad's age.

"I know, this little madam is giving me the run around."

"Would you like me to walk you home?"

"No, that's fine, I only live around the corner." I looked over his shoulder into the lobby where Robert remained by the lift.

I thanked the security guard for his concern then turned, scratching Constance's head to calm her. Robert obviously wanted me to find something important inside the offices. *Maybe his killer?* I thought. But there was no way I could get in there .

THE FOLLOWING DAY WAS ANOTHER BUSY ONE FOR THE café, and I was relieved when Lynn popped over and offered to cover my break. I didn't want to tell her about seeing Robert again, in case she suggested developing my so-called 'gift'. As sensible as that may have seemed, I wanted to do things my way.

Sitting in the snug, I bit into an egg mayo sandwich, which was my favourite filling. I had put it between soft wholemeal bread, with crisp cress and a crack of salt. I looked to the garden where Constance was sprawled out on the lawn, like a carefree lion in a pool of sunshine.

I scanned the evidence I had received so far, which was spread out on my coffee table. I picked up the keys. *What do these open?* I thought. There was clearly a lot that Robert had not told his wife. For instance, the theatre tickets, apparently Mia was no fan of musicals, even those which bore her name. I wondered who he'd been taking for evenings out. I had an urge to search his office for clues. Although, I'd need a look-out. Annie was well known in town and easily recognisable so I couldn't take her. And Izzy was the 'It Girl' of Branden Bay, and famous. Indeed, everywhere we went people stopped to speak to her. Lynn, I'm sure, would say no – it wasn't exactly the moral thing to do. Clearly H was not a contender, with him being a police sergeant. Not forgetting that he'd told me to keep out of it. So that left only one person in Branden Bay I could ask – Jeff.

Jeff was the local trainee paranormal investigator, with an extensive collection of ghost hunting paraphernalia. He'd spent most of his youth in his bedroom, watching ghost hunting videos on YouTube so wasn't well known around town. This made him the perfect companion for an undercover job.

FOLLOWING A WELCOME FLURRY OF AFTERNOON TEAS, I closed the café as the van pulled up with 'Paranormal Jeff' emblazoned on the side. It was a magnetic sign which Jeff hid in the back and only put on when he was out of sight of home. He still lived with his mother, who didn't approve of his hobby. I can't say I blamed her.

Jeff grinned at me as he walked up the path, with excitement written all over his face. He scratched his wannabe beard, which sprouted from the bottom of his chin in a sandy shade that matched the hair on his head.

"At your service, boss," he said saluting me.

Jeff had previously overheard Lynn telling me that I was a 'bridge medium,' which Lynn explained was the term for someone who creates a door between the physical and spirit worlds and that every 'bridge medium' has a protector called a 'gatekeeper.' Now did I believe this? Of course not. But Jeff had declared himself to be my gatekeeper and protector.

I took him through the house. "I've got a chicken stew in the slow cooker. Want some?"

"Yes, please."

After we finished our meal, I filled him in on the details of the case. "We need to gain access to Chesham's, but I'm not quite sure how to do that," I said.

"We could take the van and say we're part of an ongoing paranormal investigation," Jeff suggested.

"I don't think that's going to wash somehow. Maybe we should pretend to be pest control?"

"Won't they know whether they have pests or not?"

"They share an office block. We'll say we've fumigated the solicitor's office downstairs and need to check if they've migrated."

"What sort of pests?"

"Rats. We can say we're looking for droppings and snoop around."

"Great idea, boss. I could take my Ouija."

"No. I want to look for clues in the physical world." I wasn't a fan of the Ouija, since Jeff had whipped it out in my front room one evening, causing no end of havoc. I hoped I wouldn't need to go down that route again.

CHAPTER 5

It was late afternoon, when Jeff and I entered the main lobby of Chesham's office building. Jeff had come up trumps with the rat catching props. He was between education, having finished his Bachelors and waiting for his Masters course to begin, and had taken a part-time job in a large DIY store. We had matching blue boiler suits, masks, a large orange plastic box with a black handle, which had a few things clattering around inside and a bottle with a spray attachment on a pipe. My heart thudded as I flashed an ID card with BEST PEST CONTROL in bold, which Jeff had run off his computer and laminated. The security guard nodded at the visitors' book and watched as we scribbled our fake names into it. I was taken aback at how easy it was to gain access.

We entered the lift and not surprisingly, no-one else wanted to get into the carriage with us.

As soon as the doors shut, I breathed out. "Phew."

"Ace work, boss," said Jeff.

"Don't jump the gun, there's still a big chance we'll get caught." My palms were sweating and I was overheating in the boiler suit.

I swallowed hard as the doors opened at the second floor. Stepping out, we headed for the reception desk. A girl with long blonde hair looked up and scowled at me.

Really? I thought and raised my eyebrows. Having worked on reception myself, back in the City of London, I had been taught to smile at all visitors, even if they were pest control.

She gave me a look up and down.

"We're from Best Pest Control," I said as I flashed her my card. I was really overheating now. I pulled the mask down to my neck. I'd had to roll the overalls up at the bottom because my legs were too short. And I wore a cap to disguise my flaming hair. Standing beside the gangly Jeff in matching overalls, I guess I looked rather ridiculous.

"I phoned ahead, we're here for the ..."

"Vermin." She scrunched her petite nose. "I studied accountancy at university and this is where I wind up? I didn't think my job could get any worse."

"It's rats. There's a problem downstairs, so we need to check whether they've migrated."

"So you said on the phone."

I needed to calm down, if I repeated myself, I might appear nervous and fake.

"We need to check for droppings," Jeff piped up from behind me.

"Urgh. Too much information," she said.

"Dannie." I read the name on the gold badge she wore on her suit jacket. "Have you noticed any droppings around your desk?"

She stared at me in sheer disgust. "No." She groaned. She didn't look much older than Jeff, who was coming up to twenty-one. This must be the girl Mia had described as 'that madam of a receptionist.'

"We're only here to investigate," I said. "There may not be a problem at all, but don't be alarmed if you see us crawling around on the floor. Do you have any empty offices? It's more likely that the rats will be there. They're shy little creatures."

"You could try the office up on the left, that's been empty for a while. Third one along. It has the name Robert Hart on the door. All other offices are occupied."

Bingo, I thought. I loved it when a plan came together.

"I may have to set traps in there," said Jeff. He held up a rat catching sticky pad. "I can put one of these under your desk if you like." By the look on his face, he'd taken a shine to Dannie.

"Get that disgusting thing away from me," she

swiped her hand at him. "Just go through. I need to get off at half five so make sure you're done by then."

I nodded at her and turned to Jeff, who stared at me with his mouth open as if he'd been slapped in the face. I glared at him; I'd told him to let me do all of the talking. The last thing I wanted to do was to create a scene. "Come on. Let's get to work."

Jeff followed me. "Yes, boss," he said with his head lowered.

We passed a boardroom full of people, some sitting, some standing, looking front at a grey-haired man.

"There," said Jeff pointing to a door with *Robert Hart, Director* written on it.

Excitement pulsated through my chest. I opened the door and Jeff followed me in.

"Look everywhere,' I said.

There was a bookcase, a desk with a wheelie chair, a filing cabinet and a coat stand with a jacket on it.

Jeff passed me a pair of surgical gloves and after putting a pair on himself, crouched on the floor clutching a zip-able food bag.

I opened the top desk drawer, inside was a pad of blank paper, pens and a glue stick.

Nothing much of interest, I thought. The rest of the drawers were empty.

Jeff meanwhile opened the filing cabinet which squeaked loudly.

"Shhh," I whispered.

"It's empty," he said.

This wasn't going well. His office had been stripped, but Mia had only been given a few items. Surely there must have been more. Robert's ghost had led me here so there must be a clue somewhere. I turned to the bookshelf. I needed to find anything that pointed to where his apartment could be found. If the keys were indeed apartment keys. I began leafing through the books. They were incredibly dull non-fiction, relating to financial services and how to make it in sales. I opened '*How to Close like a King by Richie Cash*', and read a few lines, sighed and placed it back on the shelf.

I glanced at the corner of the room and studied the overcoat, it was heavy and not suitable for the current climate, indeed it was something you would wear in the winter. Reaching into the left pocket, I found a packet of chewing gum and a receipt from the grocery store, dated the third of January. In the right pocket, I felt a card. Pulling it out I saw it was a large business card, with a picture of a scantily dressed woman on it. She wore a leather studded hat over long blonde hair, hiding her face under the peak of the hat. Whilst I couldn't see her face, there was an awful lot of body on show. Printed underneath in a flashy font was the name 'Nadine'. I turned the card over. 'Fantasy Lounge' was written on the back with a Bristol telephone number.

Hmmm, I thought, *It seems Robert was a naughty boy.*

I stuffed the card into my pocket.

'Yes," Jeff said from underneath the desk. "Gotcha."

"What?" I asked bringing my hands to my throat. "You haven't actually found a rat have you?" I looked down sharply and my cap fell off.

The office door creaked open. "Can I help you?"

I collected my cap from the floor and stood up to see a woman, about thirty with chin length, curly blonde hair, holding a black A4 notebook. She looked vaguely familiar.

"What's going on in here?" she asked.

"Pest control," I said, putting my cap back on and trying to remain cool, but full of dread that I was just about to be found out.

"I haven't heard anything about this," she said from the doorway, she sounded very efficient, like a school teacher.

"I discussed it with Dannie on reception?" My mouth felt dry. "There's a rat situation downstairs at Clark and Butler and we're checking up here for droppings." I gulped.

The woman frowned. "Don't you work in Connie's Café?" She pushed a curl off her forehead.

I'd been busted. I swallowed, knowing there was no point in denying it. "Yes – I work two jobs."

"I thought I recognised your voice," she smiled. "I'm Sarah."

I realised I needed to disguise my London accent when working undercover.

"The cakes you sell are great," her face softened and she smiled as if she meant it. "Do you bake them all yourself?"

"Yes I do and thank you," I said, feeling myself relax.

Jeff rose slowly from the floor, his eyes darting around in a nervous fashion. "All clear here."

"I think that's us done then," I said. "Seems the infestation has been contained. Nothing to worry about." We needed to get out of there quick as I'd blown my cover ...

"Aren't you that psychic detective?"

... seriously blown my cover.

"That's nonsense, I'm afraid," I said feeling my cheeks burn. "The journalist got a bit carried away with her article. I just bake cakes – that's all."

"And catch rats?"

"Yes." I gave a fluttery laugh. "I'm working my notice with Best Pest Control so that I can focus fully on the café. In fact, this is my very last assignment." That seemed plausible.

"Sounds like a good move." Sarah nodded at the desk. "I was PA for the man that used to use this office."

"Used to?" I asked, playing it dumb.

She looked down. "I still can't quite take it in – they say he killed himself. I find that so hard to believe."

That would back up Mia's opinion, I thought. "It must have been a real shock."

She nodded her head. "And now my job's on the line."

I felt Jeff fidgeting next to me and wished he would do something pest-control-like, rather than hiding behind me like a scared little brother, which was fruitless considering he was so much taller than me.

"Is anyone going to be promoted? Anyone who would benefit from Mr Hart's er ... demise?" I asked taking the opportunity to check for motive and a possible suspect.

"He knew a lot of people. Some liked him, some didn't."

I heard voices as people spilled out of the neighbouring boardroom. Jeff nudged me in the back. It was time to make a hasty exit.

"Well, all seems to be in order here but if you do see any rat droppings, be sure to call us back." I walked towards the door.

Sarah stood to one side. "Thanks, do you have a card?"

"Er ..."

Jeff thrust his hand over my shoulder. "Here, call any time of day."

It seemed he'd really come prepared.

"And be sure to pop into the café," I added. It would be handy to have someone on the inside to question.

Jeff followed me as I headed back towards reception.

"Nothing to report," I said smiling at Dannie as we passed.

"Good." She looked over my shoulder as I heard the lift door ping.

I turned as the silver doors opened. Inside was a thickset man, speaking in a low voice into his mobile phone. As he passed us, I picked up what he was saying.

"I'll see what I can find in Hart's office," he said in a deep gravelly voice. "We can't let anything blow the operation."

I took a sharp intake of breath.

The guy peered at me. He looked gangland scary and I could see a snake tattoo peeping above his shirt. I felt myself gulp as I stepped into the lift, followed by Jeff. I looked down at the floor noticing the guy wore bright red socks, visible above his heavy-duty Doc Martin shoes as the doors shut.

"Did you hear what he said?" said Jeff.

I nodded.

Jeff rubbed his scrappy beard. "I wonder who he is?"

"Maybe someone who could kill?" I shuddered. "I wonder what's he looking for? And what sort of operation would be blown?"

"Do you think he did it?"

"I'm not jumping to any conclusions at this stage – but he's defo on our list." He was the only person on our list.

I looked at Jeff's orange box. "What did you find under the desk?"

Jeff lifted the lid and pulled out a food bag. Inside was what looked like red dust. "Evidence."

"Of what?"

"He had a pair of shoes down there. I did a paranormal investigation last week at Harrison Heights, you know the new apartments on top of the hill near the castle?"

"I don't."

"They have paths made of crushed red brick dust. Bit of a design fault, it gets blown everywhere."

"So you think that's where his apartment could be?"

Jeff nodded as he held his bag up, displaying its rusty contents. I gave him a high five just as the lift doors opened. The security guard glared at us with his arms crossed.

I spoke to Jeff through a toothy grin – the way a ventriloquist would. "Just look professional, and walk towards the exit."

"Excuse me," said the guard. "Could you please confirm the name of your firm again? I can't seem to locate a Best Pest Control on our system?"

"I'm afraid we're in a hurry. We've just found evidence of red ants." I snatched the bag of brick dust out of Jeff's hand and shook it in the guard's face. "We need to get this straight to the lab. This whole building may have to be closed for deep fumigation and there could be structural damage."

He frowned at us as we hurried out of the building, running towards the van.

"You're ace at this," said Jeff. But as he drove us away, I realised I was far from ace. We might have moved the case along slightly, but I'd blown my cover and put us in potential danger.

CHAPTER 6

Having arrived home, Jeff and I sat at my kitchen table eating sandwiches and cake. Constance ate a meal of salmon from her favourite china dish.

I lifted the keys which Mia had given me. "I think we need to move fast. I want to check out the possibility that these are the keys to an apartment at Harrison Heights, before that gangster-looking guy with the neck tattoo beats us to it. And by fast, I mean tonight."

"We've got to be careful, in case someone still lives there."

I nodded. "I'm due to phone Mia tomorrow with an update and want to have something concrete to report to her, other than finding a calling card from some dodgy strip joint." I flashed the card at Jeff.

"Where did you get that?" he asked.

"Robert's coat pocket. I assume, by the phone number, that it's a club in Bristol. I'll check it out online tomorrow." I stood up. "I'll get changed."

Upstairs, I looked through my wardrobe. I'd been wearing clothes that used to belong to Grandma, who was the same build as myself and had had a love of trendy designer outfits. But for tonight's job, I decided that I'd go with my old city clothes, a skirt suit and stilettos. If I needed to blag my way passed any security, I had to feel confident. I looked in the mirror. My red hair set well against the dark green suit. However, I'd already blown my cover once today and with my hair being a rather vibrant shade of red, I knew I'd have to cover my locks.

Constance meowed as she sat upon a large trunk in the corner of the room. *Ah yes,* I thought, *Grandma's dressing-up box.* We'd spent many a Halloween wearing items out of that trunk. Constance jumped off and I flung the lid open, rummaging inside until I found a plastic bag holding a long black wig. Although, I didn't want to look like a witch. I brushed it and trotted downstairs in my stilettos to the kitchen, with Constance in tow.

Jeff looked up from the table. "Wow you look ...er ..."

"Smart?" I did a turn with my hands on my hips. "This was the old me, when I used to spend all my days at the office." I walked over to him. "Now sit still and look in the direction of the window." As soon as he had his back to me, I placed the wig on his head, adjusting the fit until it was snugly in place.

"Why do I have to be in disguise?" he asked. "If I'm gonna be sat in the van?" He touched the wig. "Am I some sort of rocker?"

"Keep still." I reached for the kitchen scissors. "You're my model." I snipped away at the hair until I'd created a shoulder length 'do.' Jeff's face coloured up. "Ta dah," I said then removed the wig from Jeff's head, placing it on my own and reached for a pair of tinted glasses. I swung around. "How do I look?"

"I'd never recognise you," Jeff said as he ran his hand through his sandy locks which were even more unruly than usual, having been under the wig.

"Great. Let's go." I walked towards the door and Constance followed, jumping into my tote bag. "Oi, not you missy." I reached in but she hissed at me. "Okay, if you insist. But you're staying in the van with Jeff."

Five minutes later we were nearing the top of Castle Road.

"It's just around this bend," said Jeff as a large posh apartment building came into view.

"Okay," I said looking at the key fob in my hand as we reached the gated entrance. "With any luck this will work." I pointed the fob at the gate and pressed the button. The gates began to open. "Yes. Jeff, you're a genius."

As we entered the car park, the van crunched on the gravel and I spotted the red dusty paths that Jeff had so correctly identified. “You said you came here for a paranormal investigation? But this is a modern apartment block.”

“Yes, someone reported seeing a woman from the Tudor times, they inhabited the town years ago. That’s when the castle was built. Not that we found anything.” Jeff killed the van’s engine. “The parking spaces here are allocated. I’ll have to leave the van in the street. Are you sure you don’t want me to come with you?”

“No, that’s fine. Wait on the road and text me if you see anyone enter the gates. By the looks of it there are only twelve apartments. It won’t take me long to find the right one.”

“How are you going to know which it is?”

I shrugged. “I’ll try the locks on all of the doors.”

“But what if he was sharing it with someone and they’re still in there?”

Jeff had a point.

“If the key fits, I’ll knock first to make sure no-one’s in.”

“Be careful.”

I jumped from the van and wobbled in my stilettos on the red dusty gravel. I pulled on a pair of Grandma’s black leather gloves. It was only as I reached the door that I felt Constance at my feet.

“I told you to wait in the van.” I glanced to the gate which was already closing with Jeff’s van disappearing from view. I put my bag down for her to jump inside. "You'd better be quiet, Connie cat," I whispered to her.

I put the key in the outside lock and opened the main entrance door. There was an empty reception desk.

Great, I thought. The building was probably looked after by a nine-to-five caretaker. I looked up and saw the CCTV cameras and squeezed the top of my bag in case Constance was tempted to jump out. There were four apartments on each level; and I decided to start on the top floor and work my way down. I took the stairs, not wanting to meet anyone in the lift.

Once on the top floor I walked towards the first door. I could hear a television blaring out and decided to leave that one until last. I reached the next door and slipped the key in, it didn't turn. My palms felt hot inside the gloves as I removed the key. I listened at the next door, no sound but again, the key did not fit, neither did it fit the remaining door on that floor. I took the stairs to the middle floor. I listened to the first door I came to. No sound. I put the key in the lock and twisted it.

The key turned. *Bingo,* I thought as I pulled it out and stood up straight before ringing the doorbell. A soft ding-dong sound came from inside. When there was no reply, I knocked gently just to make sure. Again, no answer. My heart thumped as I put the key back in the lock. The door gave a loud squeak as I eased it open. I peered down the corridor each way, scared that

I had brought attention to myself, but no-one appeared. Slipping inside, I put the heavy door on the latch, in case I needed to make a hasty retreat. Constance jumped out of my bag, exploring the apartment with her nose to the ground.

You'd think she was a blinking sniffer dog, I thought. My cat definitely had an identity crisis.

I removed my tinted glasses and popped them into my bag. Scanning the room, I saw a small dining table, upon which was a sorry looking, half-eaten meal with crusty baked beans covered in a green mould.

Eeew, I thought.

I relaxed slightly; it didn't look as if anyone had been in the apartment since Robert had come to his watery end. I moved to the kitchen area. It had modern units with shiny midnight blue cupboards and drawers with brushed copper handles. Piled in the corner of the floor were a few take-out boxes, although they were plain brown and unmarked – like those you would get if asking a restaurant for a doggy bag. I opened the kitchen cupboards. There was not much to see in there, apart from condiments and a few tins of soup and baked beans. Robert was obviously no home chef. Inside the kitchen drawers there were minimal utensils. Turning my nose up at a loaf of bread festering on the worktop, I glanced back at the main living space noticing how the lights twinkled in the distance from the prom through the large windows. If this was a love nest it was a pretty idyllic one. Walking towards a low coffee table I found a framed photograph of Robert and a dark-haired woman. I picked it up and shoved it into my bag.

Constance meowed.

"Shhh," I wagged my finger at her as she headed for the bedroom.

I decided to check out the bathroom. Inside was a toilet and a large, walk-in, rainfall shower with a separate hose to wash yourself down with. Inside the vanity unit I found beard trimming apparatus, aftershave, soaps and various other male personal care products. Upon the sink was a cup with two toothbrushes inside. I whipped out my phone and took a picture. It looked to me as if he was definitely living here alone but possibly had an occasional overnight guest – I assumed that was the woman in the photo.

Next, I moved to the bedroom. The bed was made. I pulled open the bedside table and inside was a mobile phone. It had a small screen and buttons, not a smartphone and as I turned it on, I was surprised to see it still had charge. That was the benefit of old-style phones, I thought remembering when I was a kid only charging mine up once a week. I stuffed it into my tote bag. I was just about to open the wardrobe when I heard the squeak of the heavy front door opening. My ears began to ring with a high-pitched noise, as if warning me of trouble. My heart burned anticipating danger. Constance dived under the bed.

Good idea, I thought as I followed her.

I lay underneath the wooden slats, holding my breath, with my gloved hand over my face as if I didn't trust myself not to scream. I heard someone opening the drawers in the kitchen, just as I had done. I wished I'd grabbed one of the knives. My mobile lit up in my bag and I saw the preview of a message from Jeff.

Car has entered car park.

I shook my head as I thought — *it's a bit late for that warning.*

Palpitations danced in my chest. If someone had killed Robert – maybe that same person would kill me? I heard footsteps walking towards me. I looked to my right and squinted as I saw a pair of dark large shoes and red socks. I knew I'd seen those socks recently. *Gangster Man.* Was it him? The thug I'd seen earlier at Chesham's offices?

He spoke in a thick growl. "I'm in the apartment right now. The door was on the latch." He paused. "Not yet, give me a chance." As I was listening to only one side of the conversation, I guessed he must be talking to another member of his gang on the phone. I heard him check the bedside drawer. Opening then slamming it shut.

My body jolted as I kept my hand placed firmly over my mouth.

"That phone must be here somewhere. It wasn't in his office." He pulled the covers off the bed. "Smith – if you don't get off my case, Hart won't be the only one who winds up dead."

This sounded bad. Really bad. I made a mental note of the name Smith.

Gangster Man gave a low sinister laugh. "You can do the next job." He paused. "No. Pope is mine."

I shut my eyes. I was going to get caught or worse, I swallowed.

"Try calling it on another line and keep this one open." I heard him say.

I stared at my bag, my heart in my mouth, until sure enough Robert's phone lit up.

CHAPTER 7

From under Robert's bed, I heard the phone. Thankfully it was making a muffled vibration sound, rather than a ringtone as it was on silent. I slowly leaned into my bag and eased it out - stuffing it in my suit jacket to muffle the sound of the vibration further.

"I can hear something under the bed."

Staring at Constance, I mumbled my final prayers. Just as I thought the game was up, Constance flew away from me and with a searing meow clasped onto Gangster Man's leg, then lowered down and chomped into his red sock covered ankle.

He swore loudly followed by, "Gerroff."

From where I lay, I could see Constance hanging on for dear life as he shook his leg.

"There's a cat going wild at me. Must be Hart's. Probably been stuck in here for three weeks. I'm surprised it's still alive, no wonder it's trying to take my leg off. It must be starving."

Constance let out another long meow.

"I don't have The Cat Protection Society on speed dial." Gangster Man swore again under his breath. "Call them yourself." He didn't appear the type that liked taking orders. But it seemed to me that he wasn't head of the gang. Smith was clearly calling the shots. Perhaps this Smith was the one that had ordered the hit on Robert.

I slid along the underside of the bed, further away from where Gangster Man was fighting off Constance and nearer to the door. I'd have to make a run for it, I just hoped this guy didn't have a gun. I prayed he wouldn't harm my little cat. I didn't want to sacrifice her to this brute, although by the sounds of his yelping, she seemed to have the upper hand, or paw.

"Just wait will you – while I let the cat out." There was a pause. His voice softened. "Come here, puss. Ouch!"

I sucked in my lips – Constance must have sunk her teeth in deep.

"I'll probably need a shot now." He paused. "I don't know the breed. It's vicious enough to be a tiger cross. Look Smith, this place is near empty. Send the team over later. I'm out of here."

I heard the front door close and heaved a sigh of relief as silence fell. I rolled out from under the bed, and pulled myself to standing. My legs trembled as I wobbled on my stilettos. After waiting two full minutes, I gingerly opened the front door. It squeaked loudly again, but as I peered through the opening, there was no sign at all of Gangster Man, or Constance, so I tiptoed out.

I hurried along the corridor, deciding to take the lift. Once inside, I rearranged my wig and put my tinted glasses back on. As the doors opened on the ground floor, I sauntered through reception and opened the doors to the carpark as if I owned the place. I gulped as I saw Gangster Man walking around the bushes.

"Here puss, puss," he said into the foliage.

Great, I thought with relief. *Constance has escaped.*

"Have you lost something?" I said in my poshest-sounding voice.

He peered at me. "No," he said and then about turned and walked brusquely away.

My heart beat so frantically I felt dizzy. As soon as he was out of sight, Constance appeared from the bushes.

"Thank goodness you're okay," I said, picking her up and giving her a huge hug. "Next time, you're definitely staying at home. Although, you may just have saved my life back there." I popped Constance into my bag and walked towards the gate. Once through, I spotted Jeff's van, parked up with the lights off and hurried towards it.

I climbed inside. "Back to mine. I have clues and I think I know who did it."

As I plonked myself down on the sofa in my snug, Constance jumped onto the armchair and settled down to sleep. I clutched my bag of evidence to my chest.

Jeff, moved around the room like an excited kid. "This is insane, it's like we're proper detectives."

A voice screamed at me, in my head. *What are you doing?* Jeff was right – it was insane. A few months previously I was a receptionist for a city accountancy firm, and now I was trying to run a café and a paranormal detective agency. Taking chances with my life, mixing with the underworld. I felt as if I'd slipped into some kind of parallel universe.

"You look a bit stunned. I'll make us a cup of tea." Jeff headed for the kitchen.

"No sugar for me," I called after him. I had to request this every time otherwise he piled in at least three heaped spoons of the white stuff.

I sat up and opened my bag, placing the picture of Robert with the dark-haired woman, and the mobile phone with the other evidence I had accumulated from Mia and Robert's office, on my coffee table.

I felt calmer once I was sipping tea.

"Look at all the evidence you've collected," Jeff nodded at the table.

I picked up the photograph of Robert with the dark-haired woman. "I'll ask Izzy if she knows her." I placed it back on the table. "I think the biggest find is the mobile phone." I pointed to it. "As I said, Gangster Man was looking for it – so it must have incriminating evidence on it. And he got one of his goons, or his boss – not sure which, to call it. So we'll have their number listed."

"Probably a burner phone used for criminal activity. But we don't want to use it here. In case it's got some sort of GPS tracker on it."

"Good thinking. I'm desperate to find out what's on it." My stomach rumbled. "We could go out and get a bag of chips?"

"I'll take us somewhere remote to have a look through the phone."

I left Constance asleep in the snug, pulling the door to, in case she woke up and followed us.

Twenty minutes later, we came to a halt in the car park of Branden Bay Castle, situated on the edge of the woods which sat on the hill, high above the town. In the distance I could see lights from cargo boats passing the bay as I ate the thick-cut fries, crispy on the outside and soft in the middle, doused in salt and vinegar. I wiped my hands on a paper napkin and turned on the phone.

"No text messages," I said. "But there's voicemail. I put the phone onto speaker.

"You have one new message and one saved message. First new message received Saturday first of June at three ten p.m." We heard a woman's voice. She had an accent, which I guessed was Italian. "You were seen romancing a long-haired blonde on the prom. No man makes a fool of me. It's over Robert. Don't bother to call."

"Maybe that's the woman in the photo I collected?" I pictured it in my mind. "She could be Italian? And the first of June, I'm sure that was the night before Robert's body was found washed up on the beach."

"First saved message received thirty first of May at ten twenty two p.m." A gruff voice shouted over thumping music. "You better sort my money out, Hart. Call me by noon tomorrow, else you're a dead man."

I dropped my jaw. "I bet that's Gangster Man. No wonder he was after the phone. He clearly wants to destroy the evidence. He said he'd kill him – maybe he carried out his threat?"

"End of messages."

I handed the phone to Jeff. "Can you check for the numbers?"

"Sure," he said taking it from me. After a few seconds he spoke again. "No record of incoming calls, so they must have withheld their numbers and there's nothing in his address book or any record of people he contacted."

"Hmmm, he kept it clean – I guess he used this phone for his dealings with Gangster Man and his mistress?"

"I'll turn it off. We don't want anyone tracing it back

to your house." Jeff removed the battery and SIM card before handing it back to me.

I wasn't looking forward to updating Mia on the case. Firstly, there was a calling card from a strip club, and secondly a mistress he seemed to be sharing a secret apartment with, then another long-haired blonde he may also have been out with. Not forgetting the potential dodgy dealings with a gangster. I shuddered. it was one thing being petrified of ghosts but at that moment it was the thought of a living, breathing gangster that scared me the most.

It was the day of Robert's memorial service. He was being buried back in Devon, which would only be attended by close family, but Mia had planned a service in Branden Bay for his work colleagues, associates and friends to attend. I'd briefly updated her on the telephone, to let her know I'd found the apartment but I left the part out about it being a suspected love nest. Mia suggested I went along to the service and 'people watched.' While it was a great idea, I had limited knowledge of who was who around town. I knew a few of the women from the ladies' society, and the regulars at the café, but most of the people I came into contact with were day trippers. I'd literally seen a sea of faces over the past few weeks and I'd never be able to place any of them. What I needed to do was call in someone who knew everyone, and that ideal someone was the 'It Girl' of Branden Bay, Izzy. I arranged to meet her at the church because it was closer to her swanky apartment, situated in Upper Ashcombe Road, where all the well-off lived.

As per usual, Constance followed me as I left the house. She often gave up when I entered the High Street, especially if it was busy, however, as I neared the church Constance was still by my side. I had a black Louboutin tote, and whilst it was big enough for Constance to hide in, I didn't want it full of cat hair. Running short of funds, I was considering selling it online. "I really can't take you inside the church. You'll have to wait here," I said wagging my finger at her.

Constance meowed at me and jumped onto the stone church wall. I stood up and smoothed down, my black shift dress, which I had covered with a black waist length jacket. I glanced around for Izzy and as soon as I saw her, I regretted my choice of 'plus one'. She looked as if she'd stepped off the set of My Fair Lady, right in the middle of the race course scene. Her tall figure was covered in black lace with a hat so huge it looked like aliens from the planet 'Feather Boa' had landed on her head. Dark plumes fluttered in the wind as she shook hands with the mourners with her gloved hands. As I approached, I could hear her.

"Robert was such a darling man and an incredible loss. If only he'd reached out to me. Maybe I could have changed his mind." She spotted me. I scowled at her as she gave me an only slightly noticeable wink.

As I got close, I hissed at her. “What part of discreet did you not understand?”

She turned around to face me. “Darling, everyone knows me. And if I’m going to be writing a piece on you solving his murder, I’ll need to speak to people about Robert. Did you expect me to sit at the back? Hiding behind the order of service?”

“Keep your voice down,” I whispered.

She pouted and lowered her voice. “I’ll be useful out in the open, darling – collecting clues.”

I shook my head, wishing I’d gone alone. “I’m supposed to be here under the radar. Everyone’s looking at me now because I’m standing next to you.”

“I’ll just pretend you’re my girlfriend, here to support me.” She proffered her arm and I took a deep breath as I looked at the open door of the church. *Here goes,* I thought.

CHAPTER 8

Izzy and I entered the church, as if it was our wedding day. All heads turned as she glided down the aisle, gracefully waving to people she knew. I walked by her side, shoulders drooping, head down. Next to Izzy, the black swan, I felt like a stumpy moorhen. Lifting my head, I caught Mia's disapproving stare. Her instructions to me had been clear: *keep a low profile.* She shook her head.

Izzy found us an empty stretch of pew, which was on our left and I went in first, sitting myself next to the wall. We were only a couple of rows from the front. I heard voices behind grumbling as Izzy sat down, there would be no view for them over her headgear. With Robert being buried back in Devon, there was no coffin, instead a huge picture of him was placed in between a couple of large vases filled with white lilies. He'd certainly been a handsome man. Indeed, if he was younger, he would have resembled the sort of guy I used to go out with myself. Smart, in a nice suit and well-groomed.

"And we begin with prayer," said the vicar.

I lowered my head and shut my eyes, breathing in deeply. Being in a quiet room with many people gave me a weird sense of connection, as if I could feel the other people's various emotions seeping into my body. I felt restless. I guess this was all part and parcel of being a medium. *Uh oh,* I thought, feeling static snake up my backbone. As the vicar spoke, I wondered how many ghosts hung around the old church. I shivered and kept my eyes shut. I didn't want to open them and see spirits floating around the room.

"Today we meet to celebrate the life of Robert Hart who touched so many lives."

Yes quite a few by the looks of it, I thought. Static reached my neck and I felt a cool breeze waft around my face.

"We're not here to judge, we're here to love ..."

There was a knocking sound. I opened my eyes and looked to the back of the church. I gasped as the door thrashed open as if caught in a gust of wind. There, standing in the centre of the entrance, was Robert, looking directly at me. I felt a blast of electricity and yelped as it took my breath away.

The vicar stopped and the mourners turned their heads towards the door. Next to Robert's ghost was

Constance, her back arched as she hissed, looking up at him.

Izzy turned to me and in a loud voice said, "Isn't that your adorable cat, darling?"

It was clear to me that no-one else could see Robert – just Constance, hissing in the doorway.

The vicar frowned. "Could someone please shut the door and get rid of that cat?"

Robert stared at me, then turned and lifted his arm. I strained to see who he was pointing at, but all I got was a mouthful of feathers from Izzy's blinking hat. He pointed to the right side of the congregation, not the left side where we were sitting. I looked back at Robert. He fizzled away before my eyes as two men got up and shut the doors. I trembled, as I always did after seeing his ghost. I hated it. Hated the physical feeling, hated the emotions which zapped into my body and hated the whole spookiness of it.

The vicar continued with the service. I took deep breaths to calm myself down – all the time realising that the killer was sitting in the church on the other side of the room. I really needed to get a look at who was there. I knew instinctively Robert had pointed them out. They were in the church and this was my biggest lead yet – I couldn't blow it. With no static left in my body, I knew Robert was no longer present.

"Let us stand for our first hymn." The vicar sneezed.

I stood up and felt the familiar rub of fur around

my legs. I pointed at my bag but Constance didn't jump in.

As the organ music piped out, I strained to see who was sitting on the other side of the church, but Izzy blocked any hope of a view. I was six people deep from the aisle. So far, I'd not seen anyone other than Mia that I could identify. I was desperate – how was I going to do this?

After three verses of All Things Bright and Beautiful, the singing stopped.

"Please be seated," said the vicar.

I heard a short grumpy meow as I clipped Constance with my bottom. The vicar ran through the major events of Robert's life. Izzy took her smartphone out of her bag and put it on her lap, setting it to record. Obviously taking notes for her news item. I meanwhile peeked through her hat. There was Mia, of course on the front row, but I did not recognise anyone she was sitting with. I could see Robert's work colleagues behind her. There was the sulky receptionist Dannie and Robert's PA Sarah behind her, and a few seats away was the grey-haired man I recognised from Chesham's boardroom meeting. I was pretty sure he was the guy in the picture Mia gave me, which would make him the managing director, Graham. Behind him was a row of middle aged ladies. My eyes were drawn to the back where a big bloke sat.

My mouth went dry. It was Gangster Man. I put a hand up to my face, and my heart thumped hard in my chest. I needed to see who else was on that side of the church.

The vicar sneezed again. "If there is anyone here who would like to come up and say a few words?" He rubbed his nose.

Without thinking I stood up. "I will." This would be an ideal opportunity. *Oh my days,* I thought, suddenly realising what I'd done. Those in my row stood up, allowing me to pass. As I went, Izzy gave me an approving wink. Mia bore a hole into the side of my head with her eyes, which I could literally feel the heat off. I realised I was going so off-piste and at this rate I'd be getting the sack and my shiny new coffee machine was becoming less likely. But I had to get a good look at who was sitting on that side of the church before everyone left.

I reached the lectern, realising I'd never met Robert. What on earth was I going to say? I hadn't even been listening when the vicar had talked about his life story because I'd been checking out the congregation, knowing I could listen back to Izzy's recording later.

I took a deep breath. "I have a poem." I didn't of course have a poem and realised I'd have to make one up on the hoof. I'd been great at improvisation in my drama classes.

Mia stared at me with her mouth open.

I took a deep breath. "Too soon you were taken, too soon." I looked into the congregation, right into the eyes of Gangster Man. They were in a slit. Surely, he wouldn't recognise me. I wasn't wearing the blue boiler suit and cap I wore to Chesham's, or the tinted glasses, and black wig I'd worn at the apartment block.

I hesitated, racking my mind for the next line. "I'll think of you when I look to the moon." *Well it rhymes,* I thought. Dannie, from reception, dabbed her eyes with a tissue.

"And when I gaze up to the sky ..." I checked out his PA, Sarah, she had her eyebrows raised. She obviously realised I'd never met Robert before.

"I'll think Robert, oh Robert, why did you die?" There was a whimper from the third row. I saw a woman with long dark hair, wearing sunglasses, I wondered whether she was the lover shown in the photograph.

"Forever the gent, kind and rarely uncouth." I gazed over the sea of faces, there were too many to remember. Robert's ghost could have been pointing at any one of them, someone I hadn't even met yet. *Here goes nothing,* I thought.

"I think you were murdered and that's the truth."

There were gasps from the congregation. I attempted to pick out any super shocked faces, but they were all super shocked. I saw a woman in the second-row mouthing, *disgusting.* A frantic clap came from the other side of the church, it was Izzy. Slowly people joined in, hesitant a first. Thinking of Izzy and her selfie obsession, I whipped my smartphone out of my pocket and then faced away from the mourners, towards the vicar. I took a selfie fitting in as much of the congregation as I could.

The vicar gave what I can only describe as a horrified expression.

"One for the album," I said to him as I popped my phone back in my pocket. I made my way back to my seat avoiding Mia's gaze. When I got there, Constance meowed.

"Darling, that was pure genius," Izzy whispered.

But I realised I'd probably put myself in a lot of danger.

After the conclusion of the service Mia stood at the door of the church with the vicar and shook hands with everyone as they left. My palms felt hot as I approached.

I smiled at Mia. "Please accept my condolences."

She spoke between her teeth. "You'd better have done that for good reason."

I nodded. "It was. I promise," I whispered as I gave her an air kiss.

"I'll see you at the wake," she said.

I turned to the vicar. "Great service."

He gave me a half smile. Constance poked her head out of my bag. The vicar sneezed as I hurried away, overhearing him say something about antihistamines.

Outside, I found Izzy chatting away to a group of admiring men. She waved me over. "Becky, Greg here is an absolute darling. He'll give us a lift up to Millar's."

Greg gazed adoringly at Izzy, even though he clearly had no possible hope of winning her heart. "I'll get the car," he said.

Izzy turned to me. "The murder-suggesting poem was inspired. The selfie move was pure genius."

I looked around to make sure no one was in listening distance. "I saw him."

"Who? The murderer?"

"Robert. When the wind blew the door open. He was standing beside Constance."

"This is amazing." She whipped out her mobile and switched on her voice recorder, lifting it to her mouth. "I witnessed the supernatural in action." She glanced back at me. "Let me see the picture you took."

I pulled it up on my mobile phone and passed it to her.

"But you only got half of the people in sweetie."

"Robert pointed to the right-hand side of the church but I couldn't see who he was specifically pointing at." I didn't add *because your daft hat was in the way.* "Which is why I took the picture."

"This is so exciting. Send the pic to my email and I'll identify as many as I can."

I whizzed the picture off to Izzy from my mobile. I heard a gruff voice. I looked up. There was a bald guy on the phone, I wasn't sure if I'd heard his voice somewhere before. Maybe he'd been in for cake. But it wasn't just him that caught my eye, it was Gangster Man, standing some distance away, staring at him.

Constance poked her head out of my bag and hissed.

I pushed her down with my hand. "Izzy. Who's that guy on the phone?" I asked.

"Not someone you'd want to get to know darling. It's Nick Pope, he used to own Branden Bay's short-lived nightclub. It was shut down due to illegal activities."

Gangster Man had mentioned a 'Pope' on his call to Smith. *O.M.G he had said to leave Pope to him, I thought.* Was I witnessing his next hit?

Izzy continued. "He still has his club in Bristol though. It's the sleazy type, sweetie – certainly not the sort of place for you and I."

"And him? The scary guy leaning against the wall?" I pointed at Gangster Man, noticing my hand shake.

Izzy frowned. "Don't think I've seen him before."

Nick Pope ended his call and walked away. Gangster Man watched him for a short while before following. I took a step forward but Izzy put a restraining hand on my arm.

"No, Becky. You can't trail them – you could get hurt."

I watched as my number one suspect, Gangster Man, disappeared out of sight following Nick Pope and a feeling of dread washed over me. How long would Nick Pope remain alive?

CHAPTER 9

After we'd settled in Greg's car, I whipped out my phone, pulling up the picture I'd taken in the church. I zoomed into the face of Gangster Man. He looked mean, really mean.

I shuddered as I showed the picture to Izzy. "This is a close up of the guy I pointed out earlier, are you sure you haven't seen him before?"

She frowned and shook her head. "Definitely not, darling. I'd remember that unfortunate face. He's certainly not a local."

"He's my prime suspect and it's the third time I've spotted him."

"He looks like a bad boy. You be careful, sweetie. Maybe you should ask H? He might be a known crook, especially if he's associated with Nick Pope."

"What's Nick Pope into?"

"Pretty much anything that's dodgy, darling."

Greg kindly drove via the cafe so I could pop Constance back to the house and lock her in the snug. Lynn was doing an amazing job at holding the fort. I told her I would be back in roughly an hour.

Greg stopped his car at the hotel's covered entrance and rushed around to help Izzy out – her hat made it a tricky process. I clambered out behind her. He said he would park up and see us in there. Millar's was a swanky hotel perched on the right-hand side of the bay, part way up the hill. The lobby had black and white checkered floor tiles. Standing before huge wooden doors to the events room, was a sign with *Robert Hart's Reception,* written on it.

"This is beautiful," I said. I'd been into Millar's leisure club before, which held a spa, gym, bar and small restaurant, but hadn't accessed the hotel from the main entrance for years. Not since I'd been here with Grandma when she'd brought me for a posh afternoon tea on my thirteenth birthday.

A steady stream of people flowed in behind us, as we congregated, waiting for the function room doors to open. I felt someone tap me on the back of my head. I turned around but couldn't spot anyone trying to get my attention. *Hope it wasn't another ghost,* I thought as I shuddered and pushed the thought of spirits out of my mind.

My eyes rested on the woman I thought was Robert's lover. "What about her?" I pointed her out to

Izzy. "Over there. The one with the big shades and long dark hair."

"Elena Corelli? Stunning," said Izzy almost breathless. "Her Uncle Giovani, owned the wine bar in the High Street and since he retired, she's moved over here from Sicily to run it. We'll have to pop in for drinks one night, darling. Lovely place. They serve food, too. I gave them a five-star review."

The doors to the function room opened bang on twelve o'clock and we filtered inside the events room. It was luxurious, with wide windows looking out to the bay and a bar sporting a massive array of optics.

I surveyed the room and spotted Elena with her glossy, long dark hair. With her sun glasses now removed, I could see she was indeed the lady in the photograph which I'd collected from Robert's apartment.

"Do you think Elena Corelli was involved with Robert?" I asked Izzy as we walked towards the bar. "A woman with an Italian accent left a voicemail on Robert's phone."

Izzy tutted three times. "Could be, I guess."

"In the message, she said it was over, after Robert was spotted with someone with long blonde hair." I glanced around the room. "There are a few people here with blonde hair." Although that was irrelevant. I wasn't employed to find out who Robert had been unfaithful with. My job was to find who killed him and I was pretty sure that the murderer was tailing his next victim – Nick Pope. I shuddered, relieved that Gangster Man was not around.

"Let's have fizz and mingle." Izzy held her hat with one hand as she leaned forward to pick up a glass. She was in her element, definitely on full form.

I picked up a glass of orange juice, I had to get back to work soon and I didn't want to get squiffy. I trailed behind Izzy as she circulated, wishing I also could get into character but was feeling the aftermath of having witnessed Robert's ghost. It always took me a while to shake off the after-effects of a connection. The room heaved with people, a lot more than were at the Church, it seemed as if the entire workforce of Chesham's was present. Izzy, of course, seemed to be taking it all in her stride as she glided across the room raising a hand in her signature royal wave. I found a good spot to people watch and leaned back against the wall.

"I thought your poem was a little inappropriate."

I looked up. It was Dannie, the receptionist from Robert's office. I moved forward and felt something stick to the wall from my hair. Brushing my hand over my head I found a clump of sticky gloop. *Urgh,* I thought. I didn't want to make a fuss so ignored it and smiled at Dannie.

"You look familiar but I can't place you," she said.

"I'm a friend of Mia. Robert's wife?"

She raised her eyebrows and I waved at Mia who nodded at me.

“How long did it take you to compose that poem?” Dannie continued.

“I made it up on the spot. Mia wanted me to say a few words and my brain went totally blank. I couldn’t remember what I’d rehearsed. To be honest I’m really embarrassed about it.” That was the truth.

“So, you think it was murder, do you? Even though he left a note?”

“Do you?” I asked.

Dannie ignored the question. “What you need to do, is to have some respect.” Dannie’s face coloured up.

Mia appeared by my side. “Is everything okay over here?”

“Yes,” I said.

The sight of Mia resulted in Dannie sloping away.

“I thought I’d come over and rescue you. That receptionist can be quite unpleasant.”

“Thanks.” I touched the back of my head. “I’ve got something stuck in my hair.”

Mia pulled a face as she checked the back of my head. “Oh. It’s chewing gum.”

“Oh no. I’ll never get it out.”

“Come with me,” said Mia beckoning me.

I followed her out of the room with a hand on the back of my head, hoping nobody noticed.

After picking up a pair of scissors from reception Mia led me to the ladies. “How on earth did this happen?”

“I’ve no idea. It’s revolting stuff. Although I did feel

something on the back of my head earlier, when we were waiting for the doors to open. Maybe someone spat it out from the balcony."

"Some people are so disgusting. I'll try to cut out as little hair as I can. I wish mine was such a gorgeous colour."

The door opened and Dannie walked in, shaking her head at me as she watched what was going on. As if she thought it served me right. She went into an empty cubicle.

"So how close are we to solving my issue?" asked Mia.

"We probably shouldn't talk about it now," I said glancing at the cubicle doors. "But I have something solid – I'll fill you in later."

"Good, I just want this nightmare to end." She looked at me in the mirror. "I'm so grateful. I feel as if everyone thinks I'm foolish. It helps just by you believing me. It's taken all my strength not to give those people out there from Chesham's a piece of my mind." She gave the cubicle occupied by Dannie, a steely glare. Then turned back to cut the offending gloop out of my hair. "There we go," she said as she lifted up the mass of chewing gum sprouting red strands.

"Thanks," I said taking it from her. "It looks like the close up of a molecule. Where's the bin."

"Against the far wall"

I disposed of it in the bin then turned and looked at my reflection in the mirror. “Does it show?”

Mia ruffled my hair with her hand. “You’d never know.” I suspected she was being polite.

As we stepped out of the ladies, Mia went off to return the scissors and I stood alone for a minute until I heard Sarah behind me.

“Hi Becky, It was a lovely service wasn’t it?”

“It was well attended.” I smiled. I wanted to ask her a few questions about the people in the picture I’d taken, in the church. “I wondered if you wanted to pop to the café for lunch tomorrow?” It would be useful to quiz someone who knew everyone at Chesham’s.

“That’d be great,” she said. “I am guessing the news story about you being a psychic detective was true after all.” She winked at me.

“I may be taking an interest.” There was no point in lying to her. I wanted to interview her anyway.

“I saw you with Dannie earlier – she isn’t the easiest of people to get along with.”

“She gave me a hard time about my poem.”

Sarah laughed. “I guess that was part of your investigation technique.”

I looked around us, there were a few people milling around and I saw Dannie coming out of the ladies room. I lowered my voice. “I’ll tell you about it tomorrow.”

Dannie scowled at us as she passed by.

Sarah sighed. “I’m not sure where Robert found

Dannie. He's the one who gave her the job. I wouldn't want to be in her shoes right now because she isn't popular with anyone in the office."

Interesting, I thought. "I've got to get off now but I'll see you at the cafe tomorrow," I said as I saw Izzy gliding over. Sarah smiled and said she looked forward to it.

"Has it been a successful day would you say?" said Izzy as she reached me.

"Yes, indeed. Thanks ever so much for coming."

"I was hoping you'd say that."

"Why?"

"I have a teensy-weensy favour to ask."

"Oh yes?"

"I've this thing on Friday evening that I really have to bail out of. I've an interview with Joanie Farrows who's starring in Mamma Mia at the Bristol Hippodrome and it's the only day she can slot me in. She's invited me to the after-show party. I just have to go, darling, I'll also meet Jamie Holmes, who's playing Sam. It's an amazing opportunity and I need it, otherwise I'll end up at Branden Primary for the summer fair."

"Okay," I said slowly wondering what the 'thing' was that I needed to do.

"So, if you could go with H, in my place."

"H?" I frowned.

"Yes."

"To go where exactly?"

"Oh, some sort of police awards night, also in Bristol. I can't do both."

"He probably won't want me there. I'm not as glamorous as you."

"Trust me, darling, it'll make his day. He certainly sounded pleased when I told him you'd be his plus one."

"You've already told him?"

"Yes, this morning, sweetie. He said he'll pick you up from your place on Friday evening at six thirty."

No way, I thought. The last thing I wanted to do was to go out with H. How would I get through the evening without arguing with him? And I didn't want him to ask me questions about my case. There was nothing for it, I'd have to wrap the case up before Friday and hand H the killer on a plate. *Hmm.* I needed to move things up a notch.

"Okay," I said.

"So what's your next step?"

"I think I've enough evidence pointing to Gangster Man having committed the murder. I have the voicemail message, which I presume was from him, saying he'd kill Robert. And he was clearly on Nick Pope's tail – so maybe he's next on the hitman's list? And Robert's ghost pointed to the side of the church he was sitting in. I've made more contacts and I'm getting the vibes off Robert's personal assistant, Sarah, that she's not convinced he killed himself either. I'm going to get her on side and see if I can get a solid connection between

Robert, Nick Pope and Gangster Man. This might be all to do with a crime ring. If I'm right, I believe that Robert was maybe involved with dirty money."

"Darling, you're a genius at this. It all makes perfect sense, with Robert being a financial adviser. This story is going to be the absolute making of me. I might even approach a national paper." She fluttered her eyelashes at me. "Remember, darling, you promised me an exclusive."

"Of course. I need to get back to the café now." I still had a business to run.

CHAPTER 10

Back home, I thanked Lynn as I took over the reins of the cafe. I insisted on paying her, considering it expenses from the investigation business. I made a mental note of the amount. My bookkeeping was well overdue, I'd not even set up a system, putting it off because paperwork scared me nearly as much as ghosts and gangsters. Lynn reluctantly accepted the cash after I said I would not ask her to help me again unless she did so.

I enjoyed the afternoon working in the cafe, it helped me calm down. Constance had been sulky when I let her out of the snug, but she appeared to have forgiven me as she wound herself around my legs and proceeded to flirt with the customers. If only life could be this simple, baking and selling cakes. It wasn't an easy job, long hours in the kitchen and my legs hurt after being on my feet all day, but it filled me with an internal energy, especially when I got great feedback from my customers.

Later, as I baked for the following day, I felt an overwhelming pressure to get this case wrapped up before the policeman's ball, or whatever it was I had agreed to attend with H. When the last batch of banana muffins were in the oven, I decided that I needed to find the woman, Nadine, shown on the calling card I'd located in the coat hanging in Robert's office. I felt she was a connection I wanted to have explained, so that everything fitted neatly together before I gave my final report to H, in two days' time. After all, Robert had directed me to his office, and Izzy had said that Nick Pope had a club in Bristol. I felt close to the truth. I had a sneaking suspicion that this Nadine might be able to provide me with the information I needed to confirm the link to the suspected crime ring and she looked a lot less frightening than Gangster Man. I didn't actually have to catch the killer myself – I realised that apprehending a hitman was a ridiculous idea.

I removed the cakes from the oven and gave Jeff a quick call. He agreed to pick me up at eight. I'd had an exhausting day, but adrenaline was pumping through my veins. I reached for my laptop and googled *Fantasy Lounge Bristol.* It threw up a website describing the place as an adult entertainment bar. This definitely looked like the club I was looking for. The font on the website matched that on the calling card. At the foot of the home page it gave the name of the limited company. I quickly moved over to the government's online companies directory. Managing Director - Nicholas Pope. *Bingo,* I thought, I was getting good at this. Robert must have been caught up with Pope's crime ring and somehow, he messed up and got killed. Or maybe he found out sensitive information and they had no choice but to bump him off. I needed to find evidence, because at the moment this was all a hunch.

I left the house dressed in the black shift dress I'd worn to the funeral. I added a touch of bling, a pink pashmina and cerise stilettos. Although, I wasn't sure whether it was the right thing to wear to a strip club – considering it wasn't the sort of place I'd been to before. I locked Constance in the kitchen. There was no way I was taking her out of town, I didn't want her running off down the streets of Bristol, I'd never find her again. I pulled on the black wig I'd worn to Robert's apartment and smiled at my 'under cover' reflection in the porch mirror. I didn't look like the same person that stood up at the funeral.

As I waited for Jeff, I could hear Constance meowing in a long wail, in the distance. As Jeff pulled up, I shut the front door and was soon in the van.

"Hi, boss," he said.

I noticed he looked a lot smarter than usual, wearing a black shirt and black jeans. It appeared that he'd actually brushed his hair, although his beard still looked as scrappy as ever.

"I've never been to a strip club before," he said as he drove along Beach Road.

"Oh, no, you're not coming in," I said. No wonder he was all dressed up.

"Why not? I thought I was there as your back up?" He turned to me. "I'm your protector."

"Keep your eyes on the road. I don't need protection – I need you to wait outside for me. You're way too young to be going to that sort of establishment."

"I'm nearly twenty-one and I've got this." Jeff flashed me what I presumed was a fake ID.

I shook my head. "I'm going in alone."

WE APPROACHED THE CLUB. IT WAS SET ON THE COBBLED expanse of King Street. Being a car-free road, Jeff dropped me off at the end of a side street and agreed to wait there for me. As I wobbled on my heels, realising they did not suit the cobbles, I looked up at the Fantasy Lounge's neon sign. It seemed quiet compared with the neighbouring bars, where people stood outside drinking as music thumped from inside. I adjusted my wig, then pulled the handle of the Fantasy Lounge door. Opening it, I saw a notice stating they did not open until ten. *Oh dear,* I thought, *it's only about eight forty-five.* I entered the main bar area, which consisted of red velvet covered soft chairs arranged around an S-shaped low stage with three poles that reached to the ceiling.

I heard a voice and looked towards the bar where a man stood drying glasses with a beer towel. "Are you the nine o'clock?" he asked, lifting a glass and placing it above him in a rack.

"Er, yes," I said. If I said no, I would surely have been sent away.

He looked me up and down. "I like your style. Different. Kinda classy. If you want to get up and practice." He pointed to the pole-studded stage. "Nick's been out back for quite a while, so I guess he really likes the one he's with. You're gonna have to pull it out of the bag, doll."

Uh oh. Nick's nine o'clock audition? I gulped I would try and get some info out of the barman about Nadine before nine and then slip off. But at least if Nick was out back, that meant that Gangster Man hadn't killed him.

"So how does this work again?" I asked feeling my palms sweat.

"He'll watch you dance. If he likes what he sees, he'll assess you out back. If he's got any energy left that is." He winked at me. "Apparently, he's with a red-head and has asked not to be disturbed. Although you're in luck because I prefer brunettes."

Urgh. I shuddered, as I looked down the corridor leading out back, wishing I'd chosen a blonde wig. There were a few doorways with glitzy beaded curtains. I felt sick – no way would I be heading off in that direction.

"Go on, then." He pointed at the stage. "Nick sometimes asks what I think. I can give you a few tips before the real thing."

This wasn't going to plan. I was supposed to be finding Nadine. She may be the one to give me the evidence I'd need to link Robert to Nick Pope and Gangster Man. Before I left, I'd printed off mug-shots of Gangster Man and Robert. They were stuffed in my bag, all ready to show her.

I walked up to the stage. "My friend recommended this place."

"Oh yeah, who was that?"

"Nadine." I removed my shoes. There was no way I'd be able to stand on that shiny stage in stilettos. I placed my Pashmina and bag next to them on the floor. I swallowed hard. I've got certificates in ballet, jazz, tap and musical theatre but that wasn't the sort of dancing this guy was expecting.

He put the glass on the bar. "I'm surprised she recommended us. We called her the puppy dancer."

"Really, Why's that? Because she's young?" I asked.

"She came at Christmas and left after a few weeks. Went off with a suit one night and we never saw her again. A puppy isn't just for Christmas. Geddit?"

"Oh. Yeah, I see."

"So, where is she now?" he asked me.

I'd wanted to ask him where Nadine was, but as he was asking me – he clearly didn't know. "I haven't seen her for a couple of weeks," I said realising I'd reached a dead end.

"I hope you're better than your mate. She wasn't cut out for this type of work. You look older. That's good. In my experience the older girls are much better – they know how to really work it." His voice caught in his throat and I gulped looking up at the pole.

"Come on, then," he said as he switched the music on low volume and walked around the front of the bar, plonking himself on a stool and folding his arms.

I pointed to a carpeted area. "Maybe I should stretch first and warm up?" I planned to wait for him to turn his back on me and then scarper.

"Nah, you'll be fine."

I clambered onto the stage as my knees shook. I realised I wasn't going to get any more information from this guy and would not be meeting Nadine seeing as she no longer worked there. It had been a wasted journey. I needed to make my excuses and leave. I took deep breaths. I decided to do a really rubbish dance and then get out of there. I certainly didn't want to do anything that would earn me the second stage of the interview, out back with Nick. *Urgh,* I thought with a shudder.

I held onto the cool metal and jumped onto it, treating it like a fireman's pole. Wrapping my legs around it, I glanced upwards, as if I was about to scale it to the ceiling.

The barman laughed. "This is going to be interesting."

My arms ached and my thighs felt uncomfortable against the metal, it certainly wasn't easy in the dress I was wearing. I hoped my wig didn't fall off with the physical exercise. It was making me feel very hot, like wearing a hat indoors. It was time to quit. "You know what?" I said, still clutching the pole. "I'm not sure I'm feeling it in here."

The door banged open and the barman turned his head. He looked back at me, his eyes opened wide and he quickly nodded his head towards the back of the club, as if to say, *get out of here.* He looked genuinely worried as he uncrossed his arms and stood up. I turned my head to the door.

Gangster Man. A voice in my head screamed at me, *run*.

"Can I help you?" the barman asked in a shaky voice.

Gangster Man swaggered into the room and I rubbed my head against the pole, easing my wig down a bit further to cover more of my face. I felt frozen, but I had to get out of there and quick. The front door was not an option seeing as it was blocked by my prime suspect and a likely hitman. The only way to go was out back. I knew there was a service road running behind the building and looked out for the fire escape signs ... *yes,* I saw them lit up with an arrow.

"I'm here for Pope," said Gangster Man.

"He's busy out back," the barman said, sounding sheepish as if he was being told off by the head master.

"Now," growled Gangster Man.

That was my cue to run. I slipped slowly down the pole, which made a squeaking noise against my bare inner thighs and I slithered off the stage. Head down, I picked up my shoes, pashmina and bag, before moving swiftly to the corridor.

"Hey, you ..." I heard Gangster Man shout.

That was my cue to sprint. I followed the emergency exit signs. When I reached the door, I found it already wide open. I ran on the cobbles in my bare feet. Thirty seconds later I was climbing into Jeff's van.

"You okay?" he asked.

"Just drive," I said breathlessly, as I clipped on my seatbelt and pulled off the wig.

Jeff reversed the van around and sped off, in the direction of home. "Hey, you look well scared." He had concern in his voice.

Once I had caught my breath, I turned to him. "They said Nadine only worked there at Christmas and left with a guy in a suit one night and never returned. So I can't prove a link there, but maybe the suit she left with was Robert."

"Could be. What happened back there?"

"Don't ask." I didn't fancy telling Jeff I'd got on stage to do a pole dance. And I needed to calm down. I thought that maybe some music would help. My heart was going ten to the dozen.

"Can you put something relaxing on the radio?" I asked.

Jeff flicked through the channels until he got to the local station, which was playing some slow sounds.

"Perfect," I said, as I laid my head back on the seat. Jeff drove without speaking. As I listened to the music, I felt my heartbeat slow. We had been driving for forty minutes and had just past the 'Welcome to Branden Bay' sign, as the news started.

"Welcome to the ten o'clock report. Just coming in. A man has been found dead this evening at the Fantasy Lounge in Kings Street, Bristol. Police are not releasing details of the victim's name at this time as they have yet to notify the next of kin. They are treating the death as suspicious and are currently looking for a woman of interest who fled the scene. Keep tuned for updates."

"What? Someone got killed back there?" Jeff glanced at me, then back at the road. "No wonder you're stressed."

I gasped. "I didn't see anyone get killed. But Gangster Man turned up. He must have killed Nick."

"You saw the prime suspect? That's insane. And now he's killed again. Maybe we should have told H."

I let out a long breath. *Why didn't I tell H?* I asked myself knowing that I'd let my pride get in the way. Was it my fault Nick Pope was dead? I felt sick to the core.

"But they said they are looking for a woman of interest," said Jeff. "Not a man."

I felt heat rush to my cheeks. "They probably think I witnessed it."

"Unless he's pointing the finger at you?"

I went hot, then cold, then hot again. "You're not making me feel any better, Jeff." I picked the wig up off my lap. "Thank goodness I was wearing this."

"You never know, it could be Gangster Man that's dead – they haven't released the name yet."

I puffed out. "Let's go back to mine and wait for the report to come in." I felt hot tears prick the back of my eyes. What on earth was I doing? This was no game – this was serious.

We pulled up outside my house and went in. I walked straight through to the kitchen and picked up Constance, hugging her to my chest – hoping that the feel of her fluffy body would stop mine from shaking.

"I'll make us tea," said Jeff.

This time I didn't ask him to leave out the sugar.

We waited, glued to the radio until one o'clock when they released the name of the dead man. Nick Pope. The police were looking for a red-haired woman who had been seen in the area.

CHAPTER 11

The next morning Mia called me for an update, she'd travelled back home to Devon. I gave her my findings based on Gangster Man. There was no need to mention Nadine the stripper. Neither did I think it was necessary to speak of his affair with Elena. I'd stuck to my theory of his involvement with dirty money. I mean, it was bad enough to find out that your dead husband was associating with crooks, there was no need to mention the affairs. *Talk about leading a double life,* I thought. Mia sounded concerned about my safety, especially when I'd mentioned the murder of Nick Pope, but that was overridden by her relief that hopefully a murder investigation would be opened.

"Are you going to the police station this morning?" she asked.

I realised I should. A man had died and I was a

witness who could identify the murderer. But I was hesitant. They were looking for a red-haired woman and I had red hair. Even though I'd been wearing a wig it could get complicated for me. The barman was clearly too scared to identify Gangster Man and was blaming it on the red-headed dancer who had gone out back with Nick. I needed to protect myself and thought it better to lie low until I had all my facts straight in my report to hand over to H. I couldn't face going to the police and being questioned – especially as it would look like I had been auditioning for a job in a strip joint. I needed to calm down, regain my strength and get my story straight. Maybe I could get the facts together in such a way so that I didn't have to mention I'd been to Nick's place at all.

"Are you still there?" Asked Mia.

"Yes, sorry. I'll be discussing it with the police tomorrow in the hope that I can get them to open a murder enquiry." Okay, so I was going to discuss it with H at the ball, not exactly an official meeting. "I know they have a suicide note but that could have been written under duress. But don't tell anyone else, Mia – especially not about Nick Pope's murder. If Gangster Man finds out we're on to him, I fear it could put both of our lives in danger."

"You be careful, Becky. I'm so grateful to you for helping me with this. And to know that my Robert will be able to rest in peace."

I was certainly looking forward to that part. Whilst

I knew he meant me no harm, it scared the bejeezers out of me every time I saw him.

I set about opening up the cafe. I was still shaken after the previous evening and looked over my shoulder every now and again, for any sighting of Gangster Man. Part of me wanted to run to the police station right then and hand over my evidence, but something was holding me back. I had a gut feeling that I was missing a piece of the puzzle.

I felt better after the morning, when the café had a constant stream of visitors. At half twelve, I looked up as I heard someone call my name.

"Hi there." It was Sarah. Just the person I needed.

"Lovely of you to come." I'd forgotten about my invitation for a free lunch. "What would you like?"

"Can I have a coffee and a slice of ginger cake?"

"Of course. I'll come over for a chat, once I've served the people behind you."

I sat down with a tray bearing coffee and ginger cake for us both.

I bit into the moist sponge. It was sweet and spicy at the same time. The trick was to use fresh ginger rather than the powdered stuff, Grandma had written in her recipe book. I'd blinked back a tear when I'd read it. It had felt as if she was close by.

"Do you miss Robert?" I asked Sarah, deciding to get straight to the point as I was bound to get interrupted.

"I miss the work," said Sarah. "He was pretty disorganised, so kept me very busy. I'm helping out some of the other advisers while they wait to replace him. But often when they find a new director they usually show up with a whole book of clients and a ready-formed team. If you need anyone at your cafe?"

"Oh, that's nice." Sarah seemed to like my cakes and I would need staff at some point. Maybe she could also do my paperwork. "I'm relying on free labour and favours at the moment. Once I get a commercial coffee machine, that should put the takings up a lot." Although I doubted I could match her salary at Chesham's.

"I really fancy a change of scenery. I've been working at Chesham's for a couple of years now." She took a sip of her coffee. "And if they offer me redundancy, I could take something on less pay for a while." She'd obviously read my thoughts. "Although they have a vacancy at Chesham's now."

"Really?"

"Yes. On reception. Dannie finally got let go this morning. She was late again. And then there was a box of extra things, which the police had initially collected then returned, which are supposed to be sent to Mrs Hart."

"Really?"

"Yes, personal things like the suicide note. And Dannie got caught rummaging through it in Robert's office. Graham fired her on the spot."

I'd like to look through that box, I thought. Mia would

end up with it in time, but it would be quicker if I could get hold of the suicide note and email a copy of it to her so she could check the handwriting, before I gave my report to H.

Sarah lowered her voice. "Have you seen his ghost?"

There was no point denying it.

I nodded. "I said I'd have a look into his death for Mia. Since she's been banned from the office."

"They were a bit harsh on her. Dannie got her back up and she went mad. Although I don't know Mrs Hart that well – not with her and Robert being estranged."

"Estranged?"

"Not sure why they didn't divorce – they hardly saw each other. I assumed she was having an affair because Robert told me she had her own life. What else could that mean?"

"I don't know." *Oh dear,* I thought. I knew they lived apart during the week but Mia having an affair? I'd been viewing her as the wronged wife. Maybe it was all about the insurance and she didn't give a jot about her dead husband. Robert appeared to be her husband in name only.

"Did you find anything when you were pretending to look for rat droppings?" asked Sarah.

"No – it was pretty empty." I wasn't going to tell her about the red dust that lead us to the love nest, or the calling card from Nick Pope's strip club. I suddenly felt hot. I needed to have a further conversation with Mia.

Was there something she was keeping from me? I thought back to the box of things Sarah had told me about. "It'd be good for me to get in and have a rummage through the items returned by the police." The could be an address book with Nadine's home number in or something. And it would be good to see the suicide note. "I could make a cake delivery?"

LATER, HAVING CLOSED THE CAFE AT FOUR, I WALKED along the seafront in the spitting rain with a box of cakes. I pulled the hood of my raincoat down as I reached the reception, and the security guard looked up at me.

"I've got a delivery for Chesham's, for Sarah Stone?" I said, carrying the large cake box.

He seemed satisfied and nodded at the visitors' book. After signing in, I took the lift and checked my reflection in the mirror, slapping on a friendly smile. I looked towards the reception, in Dannie's place was a dark-haired guy. I walked up to the desk.

"Can I help?" he said.

"I have a delivery for Sarah Stone."

As I said her name, she approached the reception desk and I held up the box of cakes. "Your order."

She opened the box. "Gorgeous," she said and offered it to the guy on reception. "Want one?"

His face lit up and he picked a rock cake full of currents and sultana's.

"Come through and I'll make us coffee." She led me to Robert's office.

Once inside I saw a brown box on the coffee table next to the sofa.

"There's the box. What are you going to do? Sense if you get any spiritual vibes off the contents?"

I nodded as I put the cake box on Robert's desk. Sarah stood outside of the office leafing through a file, on lookout. I went to the box wondering what it was that Dannie was so interested in when she got caught. There was a diary which was too big to stick in my pocket and I wished I had brought my tote bag, but presumably these items would be returned to Mia anyway. Also inside was a clothes brush and a red item. I picked it up, turning it over in my hand, I realised it was a Swiss Army knife. I replaced it in the box. I noticed an envelope, I reached out my hand, hoping it was the suicide note when the door opened. I turned to see the managing director, Graham, burst in.

"Excuse me. Who are you and what on earth are you doing in here?"

Sarah rushed in behind him red-faced. "She delivered cakes, sir. I got them in for my birthday."

"It's your birthday?"

"Erm, not today, but I've got annual leave booked so I won't be here on my actual birthday so I got them in early." She looked at me widening her eyes with a grin. Sarah clearly enjoyed being a part of the detective's team.

I lifted the cake box lid. “Would you like one?”

He frowned and looked inside before picking up a blueberry muffin. “If you could please leave this office.” He turned to Sarah. “Can you hold off posting that box to Mrs Hart because the police want it back.”

“Yes, sir.”

Sarah looked at me and shrugged her shoulders.

Oh no, I thought. I wouldn’t be able to get a look at the suicide note for some time. Although I considered it a good sign, if the police wanted the box back – maybe they were not convinced it was suicide after all.

We distributed the cakes. Some of the staff recognised me from the café and said they’d be over again. Whilst I’d missed out on getting my hands on a crucial piece of evidence, all was not lost. At least I’d managed to promote the café.

I took a slow and weary walk back home, realising I was burning the candle at both ends. As I turned onto Beach Road, I felt a buzz up my back. Across the prom, I saw Robert – he too looked tired. I gulped it didn’t matter how many times I saw him, it would never feel normal to me to see the spirit of a dead person. I wrapped my arms around myself and put my head down, hurrying towards my home, realising Robert would always be there watching, until the killer was apprehended.

. . .

It was the policemen's awards evening. I'd closed an hour early and typed up my report on the murder and all the evidence I had against Gangster Man, in a document on my computer.

I heard a beep as H's car drew up outside. As I reached the gate he jumped out and opened the door for me.

"Wow, you look stunning." He opened the passenger door. "Your carriage awaits."

I'd messaged H earlier for the dress code and he'd told me it was black tie. I had been looking in Grandma's wardrobe again, because there was no way I could afford a new posh frock. I'd found a few glitzy numbers and wished Grandma hadn't been quite so glamorous. She'd had nothing that I could wear and fade into the background. I didn't want H thinking I was going to any extra effort for his benefit. I'd decided on a black gown in the end – very elegant and long, with diamanté detail. I'd worn my own shoes and a glitzy bag of grandma's with crusted jewels.

I got into the car and buckled up as H walked around to the driver's seat. I had to admit, while H was not my type in any way, shape or form, he looked very well-presented in a suit. And his dark hair shone.

"You're driving then, not having a drink?" I asked, needing to eradicate any thoughts that would deem H attractive to me.

"I need my concentration for my studies."

"Where do you want to be placed when you pass?"

"Ideally, Bristol. It's a short commute and it would be good not to work on my own doorstep. I always feel like I'm on duty around here."

"I can understand that."

"What have you been up to then, Becky?"

"Work, work, work, you know me, baking cakes morning and night," I said in a rather hurried fashion.

"So you're not sticking your nose where it doesn't belong, then?"

I changed the subject. Yes, I wanted to discuss the matter with H and thought I had enough evidence for the police to open a murder case, a double murder case in fact. But now was not the right time. I'd tell him on the way home instead.

"Are you picking up an award tonight?" I asked.

"I shouldn't think so," he laughed. "They would have warned me about it in advance, to make sure I turned up to collect it. It's an honour to be invited, to be honest."

We passed the journey with conversation about the café and current affairs. All the time I deflected the subject away from me and what I'd been up to in my spare time. We soon reached the fancy hotel where the awards ceremony was being held. H cut the engine at the entrance and we got out as he passed his keys to the valet.

H adjusted his black bow tie. He had a bit of a 'double o' spy look about him. I was aware that he was staring at me.

"You look beautiful, Becky."

A blush sneaked up my neck. "Not quite as stunning as your original date would have been." After all, Izzy was a model.

"It's great to have you here." A grin slowly spread across his face and a fuzzy feeling snaked up my back. I looked around the hotel lobby, hoping it wasn't home to a host of ghosts.

H put his arm out and I took it as we walked towards the events room. It was a shame because I knew that when I finally brought up the subject of Robert's murder, he was likely to give me a serious telling off and I didn't want to spoil his evening. I decided to delay telling him to the next day .

The room was beautifully decorated, with dressed chairs and gorgeous floral arrangements in the centre of each table. It looked as if it was someone's wedding and quite took my breath away. H studied the seating plan.

"Great, we're sat with Brad Harris."

"Is that a good thing?" I asked.

"It's a great thing. He's got a story or two to tell. I've always looked up to him." He scanned the room for our seats. "There, see the table with the woman in the red dress?"

I nodded.

"You go over. There's wine on the table, I'll get myself a soft drink."

I walked around the tables towards the lady in red.

She was sitting with a guy who had his back to me. Peeking out the top of his crisp white collar was a snake tattoo.

I gasped putting a hand up to my mouth.

He turned around.

It's Gangster Man! A voice screamed in my head

CHAPTER 12

I did a quick about turn in the events room. I had to tell H that there was a hitman in the room, a double murderer no less, sitting at our table. Why was he there? Was he someone's plus one? I felt dizzy. H approached with a large glass of water in his hand. I held onto the back of a chair to steady myself. He was soon by my side supporting me.

"Sit down," I heard him say, as if from a distance, even though he was standing right beside me. "Here drink this," he said passing me his glass of iced water.

The cool liquid ran down my throat and I slowly came to.

"Are you okay?"

I nodded. "But there's something I need to tell you."

H frowned. "We'll discuss it over dinner." He put

his hand out for mine. "We need to sit down at our table."

I glanced over at Gangster Man "No, I need to tell you in private."

"What now? The food will be served in ten minutes."

"That's long enough."

"Okay, we'll go out onto the balcony. The fresh air will do you good." He took the glass of water from me.

The events room had large glass doors at one end, which led out to a balcony overlooking Bristol's Harbourside. I held onto H's arm as he led me there. My legs felt like jelly. *Get a grip*, I thought.

I leaned against the railings with H between me and the function room.

"Come on then, let's have it," he said.

I looked over his shoulder and took a sharp intake of breath. Gangster Man was approaching us with the woman in red by his side.

H turned around to see what I was looking at. "Brad, Hi. I see we're on the same table."

What? H knows Gangster Man? I asked myself. Gangster Man was Brad, his friend. I had to agree with what H said earlier, Brad would have a few interesting stories to tell.

H shook Brad's hand, then looked at the lady in red. "Lucy Smith. I've not seen you since our training days. How are you?"

Smith? I remembered that name from when I was

under the bed in Robert's apartment. Gangster Man aka Brad had been on the phone to a Smith. *Is she his accomplice?* I thought as my brain ran on overdrive. *A gangster and his moll?*

"And this is?" Gangster Man asked in the deep growl I had come to recognise. He narrowed his eyes.

"Becky James," said H, "from Branden Bay."

"You look familiar." Brad frowned. "Have we met before?"

I shook my head as a solitary bead of sweat ran down my back. "Don't think so," I said in an extremely high squeak. Then coughed rubbing my hand down the front of my neck.

"She owns a café on the sea front," said H smiling at me.

Lucy laughed. "Brad never forgets a face. He's working a case in Branden Bay at the moment – he probably passed you in the street."

"Becky's face was plastered on the front of the Gazette a couple of weeks back, when she opened her café."

Brad shook his head. "I feel as if I've met you in person. I recognise your voice. London?"

"Yes. But I don't remember meeting you," I lied.

"It'll come to me." He continued to stare at me.

I hope not, I thought as I gave a nervous laugh.

Brad turned to H. "I wanted to have a quiet word."

"Okay." H gave me an apologetic glance.

I pushed a strand of hair behind my ear, hoping

that no-one noticed my hand shaking. Lucy smiled at someone passing and began a conversation with them. I turned away from Brad and H and leaned over the railings, looking at the long boats in the harbour, but concentrating my attention on their conversation.

Brad's voice was low, but I could still make out what he was saying. "I'm on the murder case involving Nick Pope. I was close to shutting down his operation, but as I'm sure you know, I found him dead when I went in to pick him up. He had a connection to a financial advisor in Branden Bay. I wondered if he was on your radar. A Robert Hart?"

I gasped then covered it up with a sneeze.

"Are you okay?" Brad asked.

I turned and gulped. "Yes, s–sorry, I must be allergic to your aftershave." The penny dropped. *And you fancy yourself as a private investigator?* I scolded myself. As I listened, I felt such an idiot. Gangster Man wasn't a hitman, or even a bent copper – he was a detective on the case. I felt a hot and cold flush cover my body. I'd been so close to making an idiot of myself in front of H, again. Thank goodness I'd been interrupted.

I gave a short laugh and turned back as if admiring the scene, but not before I'd caught H's expression. I guessed he knew I'd been up to something. I knew I'd have to get my story straight before he grilled me.

H asked Brad. "Are you talking about Robert Hart, who drowned himself in the bay?"

"That's the one. The suicide is questionable."

I stopped myself from turning to give H a smug look.

Brad continued. "I see from the files that a suicide note was written in the victim's handwriting. There's a possibility that he was forced to write it or maybe killed himself because Pope was on to him. Accounting forensics seem to think that Pope gave Hart a sizeable sum to invest, of which a six-figure chunk is unaccounted for. Either he was part way through a money laundering exercise or he'd syphoned it off."

I gasped again and turned to face Brad. It must have been Nick Pope on the phone leaving the message for Robert to get his money. Maybe the laundering exercise had gone wrong.

"Are you okay?" Brad asked again.

"Yes, sorry, it's a bit breezy out here." I turned back around.

"Pope was murdered by a woman. A stab wound from a knife, not found at the scene. But we've collected various finger prints from the club and are going through the process of discounting the dancers. But better than that, we have hair picked up from the murder scene. The DNA is not one already on our records and we think it might be a professional hit – someone not known to us."

"Would a professional leave traces of hair?" H asked.

He had a point. A professional was unlikely to leave finger prints and hair at the scene.

"Maybe not, but we all make mistakes. Whoever went in there, went with murder in mind, whether it was a professional or an amateur."

A bell rang to signify that everyone should be seated for dinner.

I avoided H's gaze as he took my arm, a little too firmly. "Come on," he whispered in my ear. "I hope that none of those fingerprints at Pope's club turn out to be yours."

As much as I wanted to quiz non-gangster Brad about the murder, I thought it safer not to mention anything about Robert Hart or Nick Pope at that stage, as things could get rather complicated for me. All I needed was for them to open an official murder investigation into Robert's death and Mia would get her payout. At this point what I needed to do was what H suggested all along – to leave well alone.

H sat himself between Brad and me.

Up close I guessed Brad was in his late thirties.

"I'm so sure I've seen you somewhere before." He looked at my hair.

I averted my gaze. I didn't want to look at Brad again.

Our starters of chicken terrine and French toast was served and I felt a little calmer with the normality of the situation.

H turned to me. "Are you feeling better?"

I nodded.

The meal calmed me down. We had beef wellington with crunchy steamed vegetables. Followed by a lemon cheesecake. The middle-aged woman next to me was very sweet and went about putting me at ease, clearly thinking I was nervous to be at the event, rather than nervous about being sat on the same table as someone I had thought for days was a murderer and who was now trying to figure out where they'd seen me before. Especially when the police were looking for a red-haired female and I knew my prints were all over that strip club pole. The coffee was brought around and then the awards ceremony started.

I yawned slightly when we were about nine awards in but perked up when the highly-decorated officer announced the last award.

"And the final award is for the officer who has dedicated life and soul into the service. This officer started on the beat and was recruited for undercover work, leaving his native home in London and moving to the South West to help Bristol's vice squad. He thwarted not only two drugs rings but saved many citizens who had been forced into slavery. He came back into mainstream service and has been heading Vice Squad in Bristol for three years cleaning up the streets. It's with great pleasure that I award our Outstanding Officer of The Year to Detective Chief Inspector, Bradley Harris."

I clapped. "Well done you."

Brad stood up and walked to the front of the room.

H spoke into my ear. "What's got in to you?"

I picked up my wine and downed it. I watched Brad collect the award and thank his team. As he was talking, I saw him stare at me. He stopped and narrowed his eyes and then nodded slowly at me. *Oh dear,* I thought. It seemed that maybe Brad's memory had kicked in. I bit my lip, watching him make his way back to the table as people shook his hand and patted him on the back. How small was I, in comparison to Brad, the award-winning policeman? How ridiculous it was for me to think I could be a detective. And how was I going to explain myself if he remembered me?

"They'll be starting up the music soon," said the woman next to me.

Brad returned to the table and we all stood up.

I slapped a smile on my face. "Congratulations, and well-deserved considering everything you've achieved."

"When I saw you from a distance, Becky, it came back to me who you were."

"Did it?" I said wondering where he remembered me from. *Please no – not the strip club,* a voice in my head pleaded.

"You're the poet from Robert Hart's funeral."

I swallowed hard. "Not my finest hour."

H frowned. "Poet?"

My mouth felt dry.

"Can I get you two a drink?" Brad asked. He held out his hand for my empty glass which I passed over.

I stared at the glass in his hand, realising it held my finger prints, which I knew would now be on the police system having been lifted from the dance pole. *Is he on to me?* I thought. After all, he was an award-winning detective.

I snatched the glass back from him. "No thanks."

"Maybe we can have a chat about Robert Hart. Here's my card, call me tomorrow." After handing me the card, he took the glass from my hand and walked off.

I put my head in my hands. "I'm done for," I said.

"What?" asked H.

I stared at Brad my heart beat increased to a gallop. He placed the glass on the bar and it was quickly collected by the bar staff. *Phew,* I thought. I needed to calm down and get a grip. I breathed out. I was just being paranoid. It was unlikely that Brad had me down as a person of interest. He probably wanted to speak to me as he guessed, wrongly, that I knew Robert – and simply wanted some background info. Especially as my poem had suggested Robert had been murdered. Now I would have to explain why I said a poem at the funeral about a guy I'd never met. Things were complicated.

I heard H saying my name. "Becky, what's up with you? I think we should get out of here and you're going to tell me exactly what's going on."

As I followed H out of the function room, I felt sick. I needed to get my story straight, and quick.

CHAPTER 13

H's knuckles were white as he clutched the steering wheel, meandering along the city streets on his way to the country road that would take us back to Branden Bay. I could hear the blood whoosh through my ears. I didn't want to tell him everything I'd been up to – not all of the details.

"I'm sorry about this evening. I ruined it for you. It was lovely food and the band looked great – it would have been a fun party." I bit my lip.

"Don't worry about that. I'm concerned about you, Becky. What's going on?" He glanced at me, then ahead as we hit the country road, his arms outstretched on the wheel.

"I didn't eat anything all day and was dizzy earlier. I'm not ill or anything."

"You seemed to be having some sort of panic attack, as if you were shocked or scared by something."

"No – just lack of food."

"You own a café and you don't eat?" H shook his head. "What was it you wanted to tell me? I can guess it's to do with Hart. Seems you're not the only one who thinks it may have been murder."

"I wondered if Nick Pope did it." I wasn't going to confess that I'd mistakenly thought an award-winning policeman was the murderer.

"How did you know of Nick Pope?"

"I saw him at the funeral."

"So you were snooping around at the funeral? What about this poem Brad referred to?"

I groaned. "Don't remind me. I wanted to get a good look at who was there. I couldn't see over Izzy's hat so I found myself at the pulpit. I had to make something up on the spot."

"Izzy? I didn't know she knew Hart?"

"Izzy knows everyone." I didn't want him to know I'd roped her in on my investigation.

"So, tell me about your feelings on the case."

I couldn't tell H that I'd seen Robert's ghost – he was a non-believer of anything supernatural. A logical guy where only things you could see, smell and touch existed. "I had a hunch."

"You're not using your so-called powers, are you?"

"You know I can't stand that type of thing," I said truthfully. "It creeps me out."

"What was it you wanted to tell me, seeing as Pope is dead?" he asked.

I fished out my mobile phone, I had to show him something, otherwise he'd be on my case too long and I didn't want to admit I'd been active – really active on this case. I flicked through my photos until I got to the selfie of me with the mourners in the background. "I have a hunch that the killer is in this photo," I said as I flashed him my screen.

"I'll take a look at it when we get back to your place."

A SHORT TIME LATER WE SAT AT MY KITCHEN TABLE drinking coffee.

H looked at the picture. "There's upwards of thirty in this shot."

"If the killer is a woman that cuts it down a lot," I said.

H snapped his head up at me. "You were listening to Brad?"

I smiled. "Of course. And it said on the news they were looking for a woman of interest." I prayed he didn't ask if I had been there. "So, if a woman killed Nick, maybe a woman also killed Robert? If the police don't think it was suicide, do you think they will reopen the case?"

"They might do – after Brad has had you in."

"Right." I swallowed hard. I was hoping a telephone call would clear the matter up. I didn't want to be interrogated, especially if they took my fingerprints. "I'd rather not have to go in."

Constance cried at the back door. I stood up and let her out. "I should get a cat flap fitted for her." I returned to the table.

"Email me the picture. I'll tell Brad I've discussed it with you. He might not need to call you in. I'll explain you didn't know Hart and are a friend of the widow."

"Will you tell me as soon as they do open the case, so that I can tell Mia to get on to her insurance company?"

"I don't trust her," said H. "Statistics show ..."

"Yes I know – that the partner is usually the killer."

"You need to be careful, that's all I'm saying. She had a lot to gain from her husband's death."

"She's hardly going to fake his suicide if the policy does not pay out if he killed himself." I folded my arms.

"Maybe she didn't realise that, until she called in her claim." H yawned. "Motive is key. I'll be back in Branden Bay after tomorrow. If I'm put on this case, I'll be asking you officially to leave well alone. Right now, I'm asking the same as a friend."

I looked down at my hands. Yes, H was my friend and I'd let him down that evening. "Sorry about tonight – I totally ruined it for you."

He laughed. "Actually, I hate those events, especially when Izzy is there. I can never drag her away." He smiled. "You gave me an excuse. I'm no party animal, Becky. I much prefer one to one." He stared into my eyes and his pupils became large and dark.

I gulped and noticed, not for the first time that evening, how handsome he looked in a suit. My face burned. "You look great tonight."

He broke the gaze and laughed. "I can't wait to get this thing off."

I blushed crimson and blinked rapidly.

H laughed, then finished the dregs of his coffee. "Well, I'd better be going. Thanks, Becky and text me that picture," he said as he pulled his jacket on. "And remember – stay well away."

Normally, I would have been angry with someone telling me what to do. But I was tired and H appeared to genuinely care. I guess he saw me as a younger sister or something.

He smiled. "Never a dull moment with you, Becky James." Opening the front door, he turned and gave me a soft smile.

I took a step backwards. "Bye then."

He gave a silent tut. "Okay. See you."

I shut the door behind him.

I changed out of my dress and put on my PJ's. I made myself a cocoa and cut a slab of chocolate cake. I was in serious need of something sugary and comforting. Constance rubbed against my legs and I leaned down to pet her. I went into the snug and sat down pulling a soft blanket over my legs. So much information was swishing around my mind – I didn't know what to think. I'd been so sure that Brad was the killer. Now what? I had to look at other suspects. According to Brad, it was a woman I should be looking for. And it would have been whoever Nick was out back with before I got there. There was no point in asking the barman for a description because he'd said Nick went out the back before he arrived – he'd just been told it was with a red-head. I looked at the picture and the only red-head at the funeral was me. If it was the same person who killed Nick Pope, she must have been wearing a red wig as a disguise.

I texted the picture to H, as asked, and printed out the photograph for myself on an A4 sheet of paper. With Brad not being a gangster after all and struck off the suspect list, I decided to focus only on the women. There were sixteen of them. I recognised a few from the Branden Ladies' Society and also Elena, Sarah and Dannie. I put the picture down, praying that the police would open a file.

An icy chill brushed my face as Constance cried from the garden in a low wail. *I hope she isn't bringing a mouse in,* I thought. Not that she'd ever brought in a rodent – Constance wasn't that type of cat. I went to the French windows and pulled back the curtain. I screamed – looking straight at me was Robert's ghost. He still wore his suit but he looked decidedly ill. His face was illuminated, glowing in the dark outdoors. His eyes were red, as if full of busted blood vessels. His skin appeared bruised, flapping off in areas. He moaned as sharp static zapped through my body. Constance pawed at the window. I had to let her in, so I unlocked the door, gingerly opening it. A breeze whooshed in as she bolted inside and I pressed all my weight on the glass door to close it.

"I'm sorry," I called out to Robert through the now closed door. "I'm trying."

He shook his head and took a step forward.

"No." I locked the door and pulled the curtains. Picking Constance up, I dashed out of the room, turning on every light switch I passed until I reached the bedroom. The lights flickered. I went to the window and opened the curtain. I saw him outside – now at the front of my house, leaning against the sea wall looking up at me. It wouldn't be enough for the police to open an investigation. Yes Mia would get her insurance money and I would get my coffee machine but I needed to find the killer so that Robert would move on.

CHAPTER 14

The following day, I opened my bedroom curtains to check for any sign of Robert's ghost. To my relief he was nowhere to be seen and it was a lovely sunny morning. The sea rippled up the beach in long wide shallow waves. The world looked normal, I just wished it was.

In the shower, I gave myself a burst of energy, using mint and eucalyptus gel all over my body. Once dressed and in the café, I opened the doors, the smell of sea air lifted my spirits, the weather report was great for the whole day and hopefully I'd have good takings. I had half an hour until opening. Back in the kitchen I put together three cakes using sponges from the freezer. There was a rap at the back door, it was Lynn.

"I hope you don't mind me popping through the back gate, I felt an urge to come over and see you, lovey. How are you?"

"If you're psychic, why are you asking?"

Lynn laughed. "I'm no mind reader. I get feelings about things and I had the feeling that you were in a spot of bother. Is everything okay?"

I could have lied to Lynn but she was bang on, so there was no point in that. "I'm a bit under it at the moment."

"I'm offering free labour. I can help out today."

"Are you sure?"

"I wouldn't have asked otherwise. Most of my work at the church happens in the evenings. Now sit down, you look tired."

I plonked myself down.

"Tell me what's got you like this," she said putting her head on one side.

"I'm stressed due to the case I took on for Mia Hart. I'm tired because I'm trying to solve it and run a café at the same time. And on top of that." I paused. "The sightings of Robert's ghost are draining me."

"Let's get today out of the way and you can tell me all about it later."

I nodded. I wanted to ask about the deterioration of Robert's ghost – she'd be able to explain it to me. "Thanks Lynn you're a life-saver."

THE DAY WENT WELL. WE WERE BUSY AND AS SOON AS the customers turned up, I got into my stride. Thoughts of murder and ghosts ebbed away and I felt like a regular person again. After the mid-day rush, a dark-haired, middle-aged woman arrived. She had a fair streak in her fringe.

She smiled at me. "I've been recommended to see you. I'm in a bit of a pickle."

Not another one, I thought. "I'm sorry but I'm not a medium and can't solve any mysteries especially those involving dead bodies."

The woman raised her eyebrows. "I'm interested in a cake?"

"Oh, I'm so sorry." I picked up my order book. "I've had a few people contact me after that newspaper report in the Gazette."

"I don't read newspapers, poppet. Most of it's made up anyway. It's my grandchild's christening in a few weeks and I've been let down by the person who was going to do the cake. It's not her fault, she's broken her hip. So I wondered – do you make large cakes?"

"I'll be honest," I said. "I've never made a celebration cake in my life. I could try but I wouldn't want to let you down with a failure. But do come back to me if you're stuck, because I could suggest an alternative."

"What would the alternative be?"

"Follow me." I led her to my counter where I had a few cakes displayed. "I could make a couple of regular sized cakes and place them side by side, or make individual cupcakes with flags in spelling out the word christening and your grandchild's name."

The lady nodded. “I like the idea of small cakes, it saves using a knife, especially with children around.”

“How many are you catering for?”

“Forty.”

“That’s do-able. Would you like to share a pot of tea with me and I’ll bring a few cupcakes over for you to try on the house? I’m Becky, by the way and you are?”

Lynn came out of the kitchen. “Hi, Carol, how are you?”

“Great. I didn’t realise you worked here.”

“I’m helping Becky out – she’s doing so well.” Lynn beamed it me.

“Thanks so much, Lynn,” I said.

“I’ll catch up with you later about that other matter.” She smiled at me.

I turned to Carol. “Do you know Lynn from the spiritualist church?”

“Oh no, I don’t bother with that nonsense dear – we’ve known each other since school.”

Carol put me at ease, she had the most beautiful brown eyes, which appeared uncannily familiar. After trying the three cakes and tea, which was interrupted three times by me serving customers, Carol sat back smiling. “I can’t make my mind up – they’re all so delicious. Can I have a selection of all three?”

“Of course you can. Or if you want any other flavour, I can pop you over a sample.”

“No, these three will be perfect - vanilla, chocolate and lemon. If you could do forty for the display and an extra box of fifteen just in case." She laughed. "Knowing my lot there'll be a few up for seconds."

She stood up and I saw a familiar tall figure coming into the shop. It was H. My stomach churned, I hoped he wasn't there to drag me to the police station.

"I need to speak to you about that matter we were discussing last night," he said forcefully.

Well, how do you do? I thought. He could be so abrupt at times.

Carol swung around to face him.

"Henry!"

"Ma?" said H as he stared at Carol looking confused.

"What's this all about?" she said. "How did you know I was here?"

"I er ..."

"And what did we discuss last night?" She shook her head. "I didn't even see you. Are you feeling alright?" She turned around to me. "Oh." A smile crept over her face. "Were you talking to Becky here? Are you friends?" Her grin stretched from one ear to the other.

As H sighed, I realised where I'd seen Carol's brown eyes before. "What are you doing here, Ma?"

"I was sorting the cakes for Tori's christening. And you?"

"I er ... came in to ..."

Carol turned back to me. "Were you Henry's secret date to the awards night?"

I laughed. “I didn’t realise it was hush-hush.” I sucked in a smile. I had to admit the more uncomfortable H looked, the more relaxed I felt.

Carol retrieved her bag from the table and put it over her shoulder. “That’s sorted then. Becky, you’re coming to ours for supper this evening.” She turned to her son. “I‘ve taken up far too much of Becky’s time, she’s got a business to run. You can talk to her about it tonight at our place.” She turned back to face me. “Twenty-five Church Lane. We eat at six thirty.” She grabbed her son’s arm. “Come along, Henry.”

I RUMMAGED IN GRANDMA’S WARDROBE, LOOKING FOR something suitable to wear to Carol’s, finally deciding on a pink top and a green skirt. Grandma had always opted for simple classic styles – the sort that never went out of fashion. I love juxtaposing colours, which is handy, because when you have red hair, let’s face it – most things are going to clash. I didn’t know why I felt I wanted to impress Carol. I’m sure it wasn’t because she was H’s Mum. Maybe it was because I always felt so mediocre compared to him. He seemed so perfect-looking, in an obvious way, of course. He was a bona fide detective – and I was a wannabe amateur sleuth. So I figured he would always trump me. But I got the impression Carol really liked me and I could do with some motherly love. I was missing my own so much. I looked at the calendar – the monthly call from my parents was the following day and I had so much to update them on, but also so much I didn't want to worry them with. This month they'd arranged to give me a video call. I was so excited to see their faces again.

Half an hour later, I took one last look at my reflection in the porch mirror and headed off. I knew Church Street – unsurprisingly, it was near the church. It was a bit of a trek up the hill but I was pretty early so could walk slowly. As I neared the house, I felt Constance's fur around my legs. I'd been so away with the fairies as I walked up, I didn't even notice her there. With no time to walk her back, I decided that turning up with my cat would be a lesser crime than turning up late.

I rang the bell and H opened the door.

"Hi." I smiled, feeling like I was invading his privacy.

"You'd better come in then. Oh ..." He looked down at my feet. "You've brought your cat."

"I can leave her outside?"

Carol appeared. "Your cat came too?"

"She follows me everywhere – I'm so sorry I didn't notice until I was a few doors away and I didn't want to be late."

"Come in, I used to have cats when I was younger." She bent down and stroked the fur on Constance's head. "What a cute, fluffy thing." Standing back up, she gestured behind. "We're eating in the garden because it's such a balmy evening."

I picked Constance up. She purred and was definitely showing off. "She's ever so well-behaved," I said staring at my cat, hoping that she picked up the message that I expected her to be on her best behaviour.

"What breed is she?" asked Carol as we left H to close the door.

"I'm not sure – she turned up at my house and I took her in. She's quite young. When I had her checked over by the vet, they said technically she's still considered a kitten. As she wasn't micro-chipped, I couldn't return her to her owner. I canvassed the locals but I'd be heartbroken now if someone claimed her as theirs."

Carol led me through her lounge towards the back of the house. "She may have been born to a feral – there are so many in town. The Cats Protection Team went out a few months ago, rounded a batch up and neutered them. It was called 'Operation Macavity'. Now come through so I can introduce you to everyone." She turned to H. "Get Becky a glass of wine." She shook her head at me. "No wonder he doesn't have much luck with girls."

I'd picked up before from overhearing a conversation he'd had with one of his friends that H did have a lot of interest from women. Usually tall, tanned and fit ones. Sounded to me like he had no problem attracting women, so I assumed he didn't take anyone home to meet his mother. Maybe his relationships didn't last long enough? Not that H's love life was any concern of mine.

We stepped into the back garden where a large table was positioned on a crazy-paved patio. It was underneath a trellis, over which a clematis sprouted flowers in different shades of purple.

"Hello," I said nodding at the family gathered at the table.

"This is Rachael, Henry's sister," said Carol. "With little Victoria, who will be christened."

"Lovely to meet you," said Rachael as she cradled her baby.

"This is Billy, her husband."

"Alright?" said Billy nodding at me, before getting up and walking towards two boys playing at the back of the garden. "Come on, lads. Food will be ready soon."

"They're Ollie and Freddy, my twin grandsons," said Carol. And this." She walked over to a middle-aged guy. "Is the love of my life, Paul."

"Hi," I said.

"Hello there." He grinned at me.

H appeared at my side and handed me a glass of wine and then raised his bottle of beer to his lips.

"And this, is Becky, H's new girlfriend."

I heard H spray a mouthful of beer.

Good job we're outside, I thought.

CHAPTER 15

H stood as if on pause, with his mouth wide open, staring at Carol as she walked towards the alfresco dinner table.

"Ma, look we're just –"

"About time you brought a girl home, son," said Paul.

"Yes, a big man like you – handsome and in your prime." Carol turned to me and smiled. "And such a pretty, respectable young woman with her own business." She nodded at me. "Now come and take a seat, poppet." She pulled out a chair. "And H you sit next to our Becky."

H shook his head. I should have been embarrassed at the awkwardness of the situation but his discomfort was way too enjoyable to watch.

The twins joined us and petted Constance who purred as they ruffled her fur.

Carol fetched a massive pan of steaming paella, which she plonked in the middle of the dining table. The aromas of garlic, fish and spices reached my nose. Salad and warm flatbread followed.

"This looks amazing," I said. *What a feast,* I thought.

"Well, serve your young lady then." Carol nodded at her son.

I'm sure I heard H growl next to me as he ladled the mixture of rice and fish onto my plate. "Salad?" he asked in an airy voice as he lifted the bowl.

"Yes please, Henry," I smiled sweetly.

"Don't push it," he whispered, so only I could hear.

I gave him a sideways glance and winked at him and noticed him fight a smile. I looked away as heat hit my cheeks.

Constance tucked into a plate of fish that Carol had put down for her. The family chattered away as they dished out food and tore off chunks of bread. My heart warmed as I watched them. As silence fell when they began to eat, I asked H, "Why did you come to the cafe today?"

"I'll tell you when I walk you home."

This sounded intriguing, as if he was going to divulge classified information about Robert's murder. Things were looking up. I chewed the moist, salty rice with fish and softened vegetables. *Mmmmm,* I thought.

"Carol, this is totally yummy. I feel like I've been

transported to Spain – especially with this weather," I said.

"Ooh, we love Majorca don't we, Paul?"

H's dad nodded.

"We went there for our honeymoon. We used to take the kids there every year. Didn't we, Henry?"

H nodded and ate his food in silence.

"I'll show you the family album later."

H let out a sigh as he reached for his beer.

Carol patted my hand. "I hope you're enjoying yourself. Henry says I interfere and that's why he doesn't bring any girls home."

I laughed. "I think you're the perfect hostess." Lifting my wine glass, I clinked it with Carol's. "If you were my mum, I'd be showing you off to all of my friends."

"Where's your mother, poppet? Back in London?"

"My parents have taken a worldwide trip of a lifetime and I haven't seen them for over eighteen months. I'm feeling ..." I stopped as a large lump came into my throat.

"Oh, poppet. You miss them, I can tell."

I nodded and took a deep breath. "They'll be back for Christmas. I can't wait."

"You're quiet, Henry." Carol turned to me. "I expect he's got a big case on. He's always quiet when the job's on his mind. I might dig at him but I'm ever so proud."

H gave a small smile. "Let's change the subject. I'm

sure Becky's not interested in listening about me. Tell her about your garden."

H knew a good distraction tactic, Carol went on to describe how she'd turned the whole garden from a mud patch into the glorious colourful space it was. As the sun set, fairy lights twinkled from the trellis and lit the trees. I soaked up the family atmosphere to the point where I had to blink away a tear. I was so looking forward to the call with my own parents.

After we'd talked for a while, Carol brought dessert to the table, which was a massive trifle. The twins cheered.

"Wow, I haven't had one of those for years." I looked at the glass bowl with layers of jelly-soaked sponge, fruit, yellow set custard and fresh cream on top with slices of strawberries. I couldn't wait to dive in.

H's phone rang. "I'd better take this," he said, answering the call as he walked down the garden. He frowned, running a hand through his hair. Turning, he looked straight at me shaking his head. "No, I'll deal with it. Give me fifteen minutes and I'll be there with it sorted." Replacing the phone in his jeans back pocket, he paced about for a bit before walking up to me. His expression was what my mum would describe as 'grave'. He licked his lips. "Becky, you need to come with me to the police station."

"What? Now?" I said as a burning sensation fired in the pit of my stomach.

"Henry," said Carol. "We're having dinner for goodness sake. Stop being ridiculous. Sit down and have some trifle – it's your favourite." She flapped her hand at him.

"No, Ma." He turned to me. "Becky, this is serious. The reason I came over earlier, was to tell you that following Brad's investigations, he has officially opened a case to investigate the murder of Robert Hart. They're almost certain it was linked to the killing of Nick Pope."

Constance appeared at my legs, and rubbed against them.

"Nasty Nick who opened that night club?" asked Carol.

H ignored her.

"That's fantastic news," I said beaming. I couldn't believe my luck. With Mia's insurance claim in the bag, I was just about to come into a further four thousand pounds. I could see the commercial coffee machine I wanted, glinting in my mind. Everything was falling in to place. "That's such good news."

"Their prime suspect is Mia Hart."

"Oh?" *Not so good news,* I thought. The picture in my mind of the coffee machine was replaced with one of Mia in an orange boilersuit. "Look, I know she was set to pick up an insurance pay-out but I'm sure Mia is no killer."

"That's not the worse part." H took a step closer to me.

"Rebecca James, you need to accompany me to the police station on suspicion of murder."

Rachael's husband Billy called to the twins. "Let's play football before dessert." He chased them down the garden.

Constance hissed and I bent down and picked her up.

Carol laughed. "You're so funny, Henry. Now be a love and pop the percolator on. I'm desperate for a coffee. Try the Brazilian Roast, it's fantastic." She shooed him with her hand.

"Becky. You need to come to the station." He looked serious.

"Stop it, H. You're scaring me now." I squeezed Constance close to my chest.

"Come on, son. A joke's a joke. You're taking this too far and upsetting the poor girl," said Paul.

"They believe Mia Hart paid someone to murder her husband and after checking her bank account this evening, the only person coming up on her statement as having received a cash pay-out is you, Becky."

I don't believe this, I thought. "You know full well that Mia paid me to help solve the murder because the police were convinced it was suicide. Now you've proved her right, you're putting Mia and me at the top of the suspect list? That's utterly ridiculous."

Carol put herself between us, as if protecting me from her son. "Leave Becky alone, Henry. You've found a lovely girl and this is how you treat her? You arrest her?"

"I'm just doing my job."

"Job? You seriously believe lovely Becky is an assassin?" Carol threw her arms up in the air. "The world's gone mad."

"Of course I don't." H turned to me. "I have to take you in. We need to collect your prints and a DNA sample to eliminate you from the enquiries."

I realised I was in big trouble now because they would place me at the scene of Nick Pope's death. I felt my bottom lip quiver as Carol put her arms around me.

H ran a hand through his thick hair. "Listen to me, Becky. They were going to send over two vans and had the chopper on standby, in case you made a run for it. You can come in with me or it's going to be unpleasant. Brad only does bad cop." He looked towards Carol. "And Ma, you wouldn't like the neighbours coming out into the street to watch the show."

I gulped. Gangster Man AKA Bad Cop Brad was going to get his grip on me. "Can't I go back home and change?" My bottom lip trembled. "I've got to take Constance back."

H looked at his phone. "I've only got five minutes left to get you to the station otherwise they're coming to get you."

"I don't believe this. I give up on you." Carol turned to Rachael. "Can you help, love?"

Rachael nodded. "I'll express a bottle and meet you there."

Carol held out her arms to me. "I'll look after your cat, dear, while you're there. Don't worry. You'll be back quite soon, I'm sure."

Constance meowed loudly as I passed her over. H took my arm with a firm grip.

Good job this isn't a date, I thought. *Because if it was, it would be the worst I've ever had.*

Carol was fighting back tears as I said goodbye.

"Ma, stop with the drama will you?" was all H could say. "It's just routine."

I ignored him as he drove me. By the time we reached the police station my stomach was doing somersaults.

"Look, you know and I know that you're not an assassin." He softened his voice. "All you need to do is tell the truth. I'm not saying it's going to be easy, but you have to trust the law." H parked up and got out of the car.

I didn't move. I didn't want to cry.

H opened the door. "Come on."

I walked towards the entrance, shrugging H off as he put a hand on my shoulder.

I climbed the steps to the entrance to find Bad Cop Brad standing in the doorway – his big arms folded across his bulldog body. "Miss James, we meet again."

"I'll take her through," said H.

"Sorry mate, but I'll have to process her. You know the rules. You can't be involved with family cases."

"She's not family."

"But she's your bird. It's best if you go home."

"We're not ... I'd like to support Becky. She's finding this experience unnerving."

"Sergeant Blake. I'm the senior officer here. You know the drill. And have you been drinking?"

H backed off.

Brad turned to me. "Rebecca James, I'm arresting you on suspicion of the murders of Robert Hart and Nicolas Pope. You do not have to say anything, but it may harm your defence if you do not mention, when questioned, something which you later rely on in court."

He turned to H. "Sorry mate."

"No. I've done nothing. This can't be right. H?" I swung around.

"Brad's right. I can't get involved but I'll see what I can do."

A uniformed WPC approached me. "Come this way, Miss James."

Tears threatened my eyes as we walked into the station and approached the desk. I was determined not to crumble.

"Please empty your bag and pockets so we can log your possessions."

My finger prints were taken and a swab of DNA from inside my mouth. They also took some of my hair. Then a photo. Front shot. Left shot. Right shot. I was practically shoved into a cell.

"Why am I in here? Is this really necessary?" I put my hands on my hips.

"I'm sorry, but DCI Harris wants to handle this himself and he's just ended his shift. He won't be available until tomorrow."

"Tomorrow? So I can't go home?"

"I'm afraid you're under arrest."

"I want legal representation."

"Yes – that's sorted. She'll be here tomorrow for your interview."

I looked at the small bed, which was not much wider than a bench and shook my head.

"I'll get you a cup of tea and if you use the loo," she pointed to the lidless pan by the door. "Let us know and we'll flush it. The flush handle is on the outside of the cell."

Perfect, just perfect, I thought as I slumped down on the hard bed and put my head in my hands. *Could my life get any worse?*

CHAPTER 16

I stared at the white wall wondering how long I'd been in there. The cells were in the basement of the police station, so with no windows, I had no idea whether it was night or day. I'd drifted in and out of restless sleep, woken at times by a woman sobbing in a neighbouring cell and at others by a drunk-sounding guy shouting obscenities.

The hatch opened and a man called through.

"Your legal rep is here." He opened the door and Rachael walked in.

"How did they let you in?" I asked.

"I'm a lawyer, Becky. Don't worry, there won't be any financial charge. The bad news is, they've found your finger prints at the Fantasy Lounge and they're pretty sure the hair sample they have from Nicolas Pope's body is yours too."

"Hair sample?"

"Red hair was found on Nick's body."

"But I didn't even see him there. And anyway, I was wearing a dark wig. The barman told me when I arrived that Nick was already out the back with another redhead – so it obviously belongs to her. She's the one that clearly committed the murder not me."

"Don't worry. We have time to go through all of this. It'll be days before the DNA results come through. And in the meantime, I intend to get you out of here. But you need to tell me exactly what happened."

"Okay. I –"

"Not right now, I'm waiting for a consultation room to become available."

I breathed out. Rachael was calm – much calmer than me. She reminded me of my parents in a crisis, a characteristic I guess most lawyers have.

"H is really cut up about this," she said. "I've discussed it with him and he really had no choice but to bring you here. So please don't be hard on him. If he hadn't brought you in, there could have been an awful scene back at my parents' house. It would have scared the children."

"I understand." I realised H was probably feeling pretty guilty. I had to face the cold hard fact that it was my fault that I was in this position. I'd put H's family out and taken a woman away from her small baby to rescue me. "I take full responsibility." I hoped she did not detect the quiver in my voice.

The door opened and a uniformed officer I had not yet met appeared. “Your room’s ready.”

Seated in the private interview room, we both had fresh tea. It wasn’t anything like the English Breakfast tea I served in the café, but I welcomed it. I told Rachael the whole story from beginning to end.

“So you didn’t go into any of the rooms at the club?”

“No, just the main lounge. I escaped via the fire exit. I’m sure if Bad Cop ... I mean DCI Harris, thought about it, he’d realise I wouldn’t have had enough time to commit a murder before I fled. And what of the woman who was out back with Nick? Where is she? Can’t they check the CCTV?”

“The Fantasy Lounge is not the sort of club that has cameras poised on its staff or clients – for obvious reasons. I’m not able to discuss other suspects with the police. It’s my job to focus on your movements, not the wider investigation. In my opinion they don’t have enough evidence to charge you. Of course, I’ll discuss your points with my brother.” She smiled at me.

I groaned. H was going to be really annoyed that I did not tell him the full story.

“I’m sure having taken the sample of your hair they will be able to eliminate you and that will be the end of the matter as far as you’re concerned. And I suggest you keep a low profile after that.”

I touched my locks where they had taken the DNA sample. And shook my head. “That’s the second clump of hair I've had cut out in a week – I'll have a choppy bob at this rate."

"The second?"

I nodded and felt a chill zoom up my spine. "When I was at Robert Hart's wake, I somehow got chewing gum stuck in my hair and had to have it cut out."

Rachael sat back in her seat. "You were chewing gum and got it stuck in your hair?"

"No. I felt someone tap me on the back of the head and later realised I had chewing gum there." I pointed to where it had been located.

"And what happened to the gum?"

"It went in the bin at Millar's Hotel."

"Who cut it out?"

I shook my head. Had I been taken for a ride? Why would Mia Hart go to the trouble of hiring me to find out who killed Robert, if she was a murderer?

"Becky? Who cut it out?"

"Mia Hart," I whispered. I felt stupid.

"Someone is clearly framing you, Becky. But I don't intend to use that line of defence at this stage. The police have twenty-four hours to formally charge you. The DNA won't be back by then. The evidence so far is circumstantial. You've not denied being at the gentlemen's club. They have no murder weapon or motive and your receipt of £2,000 from Mia Hart is fully explained. And it's unlikely that an assassin would kill two people for a mere £2,000. I'll get you out of here as soon as I can. You'll have to remain in the cell while I return to the office and prepare the case papers."

My bottom lip trembled, so I bit it to control it. I needed to stay strong.

"Don't worry." Rachael softened her voice. "Mum's coming to pick you up."

"How long will it take to get me out of here?"

"Are you worried about your café?"

"Yes. But what's really bothering me is that I have a call arranged this evening with my parents – they'll worry if I don't answer it."

"I'll get it done as soon as possible."

"What about Mia?"

"She's been arrested and is at a Devonshire police station. But at this moment – you need to focus on yourself."

HOURS LATER, I RAPPED ON THE CELL DOOR. "HEY."

Someone pulled back the hatch. "Yes," came a male voice.

"What time is it?"

"It's half four."

"I need to be out of here by five, my Mum's calling me from Borneo at six."

The hatch was moved back in place with no comment.

I muttered unpleasant words under my breath and slumped down on the hard bed. The last thing I wanted was for Mum and Dad to worry about me. If I didn't reply they would start asking around. Maybe they would be worried enough to call the police station and then they'd tell them: 'Your daughter's inside for murder.' They'd be back on a plane and ruin their experience of a lifetime. I couldn't let that happen. My stomach rumbled. I'd not eaten. Not that I was in any way hungry.

A few minutes later the door opened. Rachael was outside.

"Thank goodness," I said.

It took a while for me to collect my belongings from the desk and for the police to read a bunch of legal documents about not leaving town and to be available for questioning.

Rachael put a hand on my shoulder as we left the building. "I'd like you to prepare a file of everyone you saw at the funeral with a detailed record of the chewing gum situation. Then we'll go over it together, because I think it's highly likely you are being framed and that the DNA will come back to show your hair on the dead body of Nick Pope."

I swallowed hard. I was being well and truly stitched up.

"And until this matter is resolved I advise you to keep your café closed."

"Okay," I said, wondering how I was going to pay the bills, if this was not wrapped up soon.

"Mum's making you dinner."

"I'm so sorry I've taken you away from your family."

"Don't worry about it. I've been tied to the baby since the day she was born. It's nice to be me again." Rachael gave a small smile.

As we stood on the steps of the police station, Carol waved from a white hatchback.

"Thanks, Rachael. I'll sort out the files for you," I said.

Carol gave me a hug as I got in the car, as if I was her long-lost daughter. Not someone she'd only known for just over twenty-four hours. "I'm so sorry, my darling. I felt it was all my fault for inviting you over."

"If you hadn't invited me for tea, they would have likely sent a group of officers to my house. At least I avoided the gaze of my neighbours."

"I've got dinner ready, you must be starving."

"I have to get back home to my cat and my parents are calling."

"Your cat's still at our house. I've made up the spare room. You can take your call in there in private."

"I don't want to put you to any trouble."

"It's no trouble, poppet. You're practically my daughter-in-law."

Oh dear. I thought. I'd have to explain that I wasn't H's girlfriend but I'd leave that conversation for later. I felt tired and drifted off to sleep as she drove me to her house.

I woke as the car came to a halt on Carol's driveway. I saw Constance sitting on the windowsill. Seeing my cat gave me a boost of energy. I walked up to the window and placed my hand to the glass as Carol put her car in the garage.

Once inside, I picked up Constance and petted her for a couple of minutes.

Carol came down the stairs. "I've put a phone charger in the room – it's next to the bed. You go and have your call."

I opened the door of the spare room and blinked back the tears as Constance followed me in. The thought of seeing Mum and Dad after the last twenty-four hours was too much. As I plugged the charger into my phone it lit up. *Mum and Dad calling.*

I took a deep breath. I'd got back in the nick of time. I answered the call and saw their smiling faces on the screen.

"Rebecca, darling," said Mum.

"Hello, love." Dad waved.

"Wow, have you decorated?" Mum asked.

"I'm not at home. I'm at a friend's place."

Constance jumped on the bed.

"What a cute cat your friend has."

"It's actually my cat. The one I was telling you about. She follows me everywhere."

Dad leaned forward peering at the screen and Constance sped off the bed.

"It's so nice to see you." My throat tightened. I needed to change the subject. "So, what have you guys been up to?"

They filled me in on the day-to-day work at the orangutang nature reserve and brought in their favourite orangutang orphan they'd named Becky, after me. They seemed so happy I had no intention of spoiling it with my tales of being a suspected assassin. I did however tell them all about the café.

"Darling, that's amazing, we're so proud of you. Can't wait to see you and try those delicious cakes," said Dad.

"Grandma would be so proud of you," added Mum.

I couldn't stop the tears falling.

"Oh, Becky love," Mum said.

"S … sorry. I miss you guys. But I'd hate for you to end your dream."

"Aw, my poor baby. Don't worry, you'll see us in a few months," said Mum. "We've had a fantastic time but both of us are missing home so much now."

"Yes, darling. We'll be back to the UK in no time and then you'll be fed up with us." Dad laughed.

"Keep safe," I said as they waved me goodbye.

They ended the call and I turned my head into the pillow and sobbed with my arm around Constance. Before I knew it, I was asleep.

CHAPTER 17

My head ached. It was dark. As I gradually woke up, it took a moment for me to remember that I was in Carol's spare room. There was a note at the end of the bed on top of a pair of pyjamas with a toothbrush.

I didn't want to wake you. I've left a chicken salad in the fridge, Carol x

I glanced at my phone. It was half ten. I took a quick shower, cleaned my teeth and put on the pyjamas. Downstairs with Constance at my heel, I reached the lounge and jumped. H was sitting on the sofa.

"Do you live here? With your parents?" I asked.

He laughed. "No."

"So you just pop over to watch their TV?"

"I'm here to watch over you."

"Oh great. So now they've sent you to guard me?"

"I'm not working. I'm worried for your safety.

Someone has gone to a lot of trouble to frame you, Becky, and they might do you harm if they think you're out of the nick."

I shivered. "You can't follow me around all day."

"I can. Brad suggested I took annual leave this week. He said it's complicated with me being the lover of a potential assassin." He laughed.

"Lover? What have you been saying to them?"

"Nothing, it's not only my mother that seems to think you're my girlfriend." He stood up and walked towards me. "But seriously, you need to leave the investigation to the police. If Mia Hart paid an assassin to kill her husband and Pope, she could instruct that same person to take care of you."

Could Mia Hart be a murderer? I asked myself. No, it made no sense whatsoever, but I didn't have the energy to argue with H at that point. As I walked to the kitchen to collect my salad, I decided to call Jeff the next day and go through the evidence.

THE FOLLOWING AFTERNOON WHEN I OPENED MY FRONT door with Constance by my side, H was also in tow.

"Honestly, I'm fine," I said. "Rachael told me to keep the cafe shut. I'm not opening up, so I don't need a babysitter."

"I've nothing else on, so I may as well keep an eye on you." He followed me through to the kitchen.

I sighed. I wanted to go over the files with Jeff. He

didn't judge me and was used to looking at things and weighing up evidence – with him being a science student. H on the other hand wanted to disable my mission but I wasn't going to stop looking for the killer. Not when I was in the frame. I should be allowed to clear my name. It wasn't H's freedom on the line.

"I'm going to check my emails."

"Okay," said H sitting down at the kitchen table as Constance jumped onto his lap.

"Feel free to pop back to your place. Pick up some clothes and what have you," I said in an airy voice. This would give me time alone.

H nodded. "Good idea. If I'm going to be here for a day or so. Are you sure you'll be okay? You won't go out, will you?"

"Of course not," I said.

As soon as the door closed, I picked up my mobile phone and called Jeff. After I'd updated him on my ordeal, I invited him over, asking him to park his van at the spiritualist hut, rather than outside my house, and to come in via the back gate.

He rapped on the back door within ten minutes.

Inside the snug, I brought up the notes on my mobile phone screen. "List of suspects. Mia Hart is top of the police list, but I'm not convinced. They think she hired a female assassin, who the police have mistaken as me, to kill Robert. And that Nick Pope got wind of it and was convinced Mia had his missing money, so she paid the assassin to top him off, too."

"Do you think that's possible?"

"I don't think she even knew him. H reckons if Mia's calling the shots, I could be next on the hit-woman's list."

"So that's why he's sticking to you?"

"Yes." I held up a print of the photo I'd taken. "This is everyone else at the funeral who's female."

"You should let me help you contact Robert Hart and ask him," Jeff said. "Why do you always make it so difficult?"

I pulled a face. "I'm not sure I could cope with that at the moment. Every time I see him, he looks worse, he's deteriorating. And the feeling I get when I contact him, it's like the feeling of death itself. It's horrid – I don't want to go there, Jeff. I can't anyway. H won't let me out of his sight."

"We can to do it at my place – Mum goes to bingo tomorrow."

"I'll think about it. But in the meantime, we need to put surveillance on our other suspects." I pointed to the photograph. "From Chesham and Co we have his secretary Sarah Bond, the receptionist Dannie Strickland and Laila Tilsey, who I have not spoken to and is apparently a junior director. From the Brandon Bay Ladies Society, there is Annie Fellows, June Moore and Cynthia Holmes. And then there's Robert's mistress Elena Corelli. The remaining people don't fit the build or age range that would be a fit for someone Nick would interview for a job at his club. And I want to find

Nadine the dancer. I have a feeling that she's significant."

"You don't think it's a man, then?"

"It's all pointing to a woman. I can pop to the next Branden Bay Ladies' Society meeting. They have a new president and have invited me to join their group."

"I could hang around at Chesham's and watch for any odd behaviour," said Jeff.

The doorbell rang. I sighed. "That'll be H."

"Text me that picture and let me know if you can make tomorrow when Mum's at bingo."

I nodded as the doorbell ringing turned into door thumping.

"Typical police," I said to Jeff as I opened the back door for him. Jeff hurried down the garden path and through the back gate.

I answered the door to H. As I opened it, I saw a huge bouquet of flowers.

"To apologise," he said peering between the blooms. "I know I don't have all the words and charm. But I'm sorry if I came across as a bully. It's just because I care. And I've picked up Chinese food," he said lifting up a brown bag. "

"Forgiven." I took the flowers, turned and walked towards the kitchen.

We had a delicious meal, he'd picked up my favourite, chicken chow mien with soft noodles, crunchy onion and bean shoots. I also had a few mouthfuls of beef in black bean sauce and salty egg fried rice. For half an hour we spoke about H's career and nothing about the case. But I knew it was only a matter of time before he started grilling me.

"They found your finger prints on the club dance pole," he said. "What exactly were you doing?"

I felt my annoyance rise. He was turning from concerned brother into judgemental father. "Dancing."

"So that's what they taught at your university, is it?"

"It's called commercial dance," I said wishing he would go home and leave me alone.

"I never had you down as a pole dancer."

"I'm more of a ballet and tap kind of girl," I said curtly. I took a deep breath, and then let it out slowly. I wanted to stay calm and not let my emotions take over.

Luckily the doorbell rang and it was a concerned Annie. She'd brought a bottle of wine and the three of us watched television in the snug, until I started drifting off and excused myself to bed.

THE FOLLOWING DAY, I'D CONVINCED H IT WAS SAFE FOR me to go to the Branden Ladies' Society meeting. Neither he nor I had them high up the list of suspects. I invited Izzy along and she jumped at the chance, seeing it as a journalistic opportunity. H dropped me off at the hall, which was situated near Upper Ashcombe Road, where a lot of the women lived. Izzy waited in the doorway wearing something which resembled a twin set. *Is there anything that girl can't pull off?* I thought. She looked like a blonde Jackie Kennedy, in timeless chic. If I'd worn that I'd have looked like a frump.

"Becky, darling, I've been so worried about you." She gave me a double air kiss. "I heard about your trouble at the er ..." she looked around her. "Station," she whispered. "And don't worry if they arrest you, I'll be doing a 'save Becky James' front page spread. I've already drawn up a petition just in case."

I groaned. "I hope it won't come to that."

"It's utterly ridiculous, a little thing like you ... an assassin?"

"Shh," I said. "I don't want this lot to find out."

"It does make the perfect story though, don't you think? I can't wait until it's solved. My career will soar when this story breaks."

"Oh no."

"Oh yes, darling. I've transcribed the recording from the funeral but you need to fill me in on your experience in the slammer. Pinky promise I won't publish anything while the killer is still at large. I don't want to thwart your investigation. And do tell me you're using your paranormal gift?"

"Jeff wants me to go to his house to tap into Robert's ghost and to ask him for the name of the killer."

"Seems the most sensible thing to do, sweetie. I want all the details. Although the three ladies here –

you don't honestly think they had something to do with Robert's death, do you?"

I shook my head. "It's just to cross them off my list."

"I see – to eliminate them from your enquiries, as the police say."

THE MEETING LASTED FOR AN HOUR AND I HAD TO admit, I rather enjoyed it. They'd called along an historian who talked about Branden Bay through the years. I drifted off into a Victorian world forgetting the present day. Afterwards we drank tea and ate cakes the ladies had made, and they were all so pleased to receive praise from both myself and Izzy. They treated us like V.I.P guests and insisted we took an application pack each to join. As we left, I felt convinced that none of the Branden Ladies had committed murder and indeed neither of the three looked at all like women who would be 'out back with Nick' at his club.

I bid farewell to Izzy. I had decided to get over to Jeff's I felt as if a timer was ticking and that if I didn't find out soon who killed Robert, I was heading for prison. I called Jeff from my mobile phone. "What have you found out today?" I asked him.

"Laila from Chesham's left work at school pickup time to collect her kid from Branden Primary."

"I think we can cross her off the list."

"Agreed. Then there was Sarah, she left at five on

the dot and went to the post office, then to the grocery store. Nothing of interest to report there either."

"Okay, but what about Dannie?"

"I can't find her, seeing as she got the sack. I checked social media and the electoral roll, but I can't find anything to tell me where she lives."

"I hope she hasn't left town. And we still have Elena to look at and the stripper to find." It all seemed fruitless.

"Mum's off to Bingo. Why don't you come over like I said? We can try calling up Robert."

Jeff was right. I needed to be brave and ask the ghost himself.

CHAPTER 18

I waited at the end of Jeff's road, which was on a housing estate just outside town. I hadn't told H I'd come, hopefully I'd be back home by tea-time. He wouldn't know how long the Ladies' Society gathering was scheduled to last. I saw Jeff's mum amble into a taxi. As it drove past me, I looked away. Then hurried up the street.

Jeff grinned from the threshold. "Come in, let's get straight on with it."

He set up his equipment which started going wild as soon as I got near it. With various beeps coming from his EMF metre which detected changes in the electromagnetic field.

"Sit down and do your stuff," Jeff said.

"Aren't you supposed to do a protection prayer?" I asked having been told that by Lynn.

"Oh yeah," he laughed.

After he said the words which he had read out from a book, I sat down and breathed deeply for a couple of minutes. I hoped that it would only be Robert that appeared. Jeff watched from behind his camera – he was not able to see spirits with the naked eye, but he could see where they were through his lens, which presented their energy as an animated stick character.

"There's something there," said Jeff excitedly pointing to the side of me.

I gasped. "I know, I can see him." I felt the tell-tale fuzz of electricity fizzle up my spine. "Ouch," I said as it burst into an intense static shock throughout my body. The air was icy cold.

Robert appeared bedraggled, with his ear slipping off the side of his head. His eyeballs rested on his cheeks. He was a million miles away from the groomed dapper guy I'd seen in his photographs. I swallowed as he took a step towards me, reminding myself of what Lynn had told me, that I wasn't really seeing a zombie, this was the way my mind was representing Robert's spiritual state. He was clearly in some sort of decline.

I leaned back, clutching at the arm rests of the chair. "Robert, I'm here for you. But I need help. I need to know who did this to you. Can you speak? Can you tell me?"

He opened his mouth and emitted a moan, my

body began to shake all over. I couldn't make out what he was saying.

"What's going on?" asked Jeff.

"He's saying something that sounds like role honey? Hole? Runny?" I shook my head. "I'm sorry Robert – please. Again." Whilst I could see spirits with the naked eye, I found verbal communication challenging. I guess it would have been easier if I'd wanted to develop my gift. But I didn't and as I watched him, I swore this would be the last time.

I heard an S sound, followed by an M.

"Ah, stole money. So, the person who killed you also stole Nick's money?"

Robert nodded.

We were getting somewhere. "And who was it?"

Robert stood a little taller, as if limbering up to reveal the name – as if he only had one chance.

"You can do it." I said, willing him on, rubbing my hands on my knees in an effort to get rid of the pins and needles.

He opened his mouth then a flash of light filled the room. In the doorway was an angry, very angry Mrs Myers, AKA Jeff's mother.

"Mum!" The fear in Jeff's voice was evident.

"I knew it," said Mrs Myers. "I saw you with your ginger-topped head down the street." She pointed at me before turning to Jeff. "I told you not to mess around with this little hussy." She walked towards me. "She's got the devil in her."

I scrambled to a standing position.

"And I heard down the club – she's an assassin. I got a taxi straight back."

"She's been framed," said Jeff.

"You're blinded, Jeff. She's a witch, just like her Grandmother."

I put my hands on my hips. "My Grandma was a wonderful and kind woman."

Mrs Myers pushed up the sleeves of her light blue cardigan. "How dare you take advantage of my boy."

"Excuse me, I've done nothing wrong."

"If you so much as lay a finger on him, you cougar."

"We're not romantically involved. And I'm only twenty-six?"

"Out. Out. Out." She turned to Jeff. "And you're grounded."

"Are you okay?" I asked Jeff as he ushered me out of the room.

"She'll calm down in a minute." He rubbed his scrappy beard. "She has an overactive imagination."

A crash came from the lounge.

"You better get back inside before she trashes your equipment."

"I should walk you back."

"No, I'll be fine."

I was soon out of the estate and walking towards the pier end of the bay. The funfair was open and I heard the excited screams of children on the rides. I dreamed of a carefree life. I was so fed up with Jeff's mum's interruption. Robert had been about to give me the name of the killer. I felt in my heart, I'd missed the window. Therefore, I had to focus on what he had been able to tell me, that whoever stole the money from Nick Pope also killed Robert. That was something I could give the police. Although I was sure they would not accept evidence from beyond the grave, it was worth a shot – after all my freedom was on the line.

As I turned onto Beach Road, I saw H leaning against my front wall with his hands in his jeans pockets. I fished my phone out of my bag. I'd had it on silent since the talk at the Ladies' Society. Three missed calls, all from H. *He needs to chill,* I thought. The killer was probably laying low anyway, planning their escape with the missing money, not plotting my murder.

"Where have you been? I've spoken to Izzy and she said she left you nearly two hours ago."

"I fancied a walk and popped over to see Jeff."

"You could have let me know. Or answered my calls." He ran a hand through his hair. "Have you eaten?"

I shook my head.

He scuffed the floor with his foot. "I thought we could go out for a meal. I've booked a table at Corelli's wine bar. Izzy said they do great food."

Well done, Izzy, I thought as a smile broke over my face. I could check out Elena Corelli and maybe ask her a few questions. "Great idea."

H gave a large grin and stood up straight. "The table's booked for half seven."

THE SKY TURNED PINK WITH A FIERY SUNSET BEHIND US as we walked up the High Street towards Corelli's. H opened the door for me when we reached there. He looked quite smart again. Even though he had his trademark jeans on, he wore a white linen shirt, rather than his usual tight black t-shirt.

As we walked in, Elena gave him a wide smile. "Mister Blake?" She had a soft and attractive Italian accent.

"Yes." H nodded. "Thanks for letting us have a table at short notice."

"I've reserved a place by the window." She motioned us to a very romantic-looking table for two with a lit candle and a single red rose in a slimline vase. I heard the music of ABBA playing softly in the background. As we took our seats. she fetched the menus, which were large one-page sheets. "The specials today are lobster linguine and roasted tomato and pesto tart."

"Thank you," I said feeling a warmth spread over my body.

"I'll be over shortly to take your drinks order."

I watched as Elena walked up to the bar. She was elegant and classy. It was easy to see how Robert had fallen for her. I shook my head, I had no idea what the situation had been between Mia and Robert. I did hope that I had not been duped by Mia. Seeing Elena up close, she did not seem the sort to commit murder and certainly not the type to stab Nick Pope to death.

"It's so nice in here, I wish I could relax long enough to enjoy it." I sighed.

H pushed his hand across the table and touched mine.

I jumped as a zing of static shot through my hand.

He smiled "Things will get better. You have to trust the law – it will all work out right in the end."

"But maybe not until after I have to do a stint in jail when that DNA from my hair turns up."

"I'm doing all I can. Hang in there."

After we'd placed our orders and Elena had brought our drinks, I glanced at H. Light from the candle flickered reflecting in his eyes. He was smiling at me an awful lot.

"Is everything okay?" I took a sip of my drink.

"I thought it would be nice to get away from the house and have an evening together without distractions."

I nodded and looked around. "It's lovely in here."

"And I have a gift for you." He reached for the pocket in his shirt and took out a small envelope. "Here." He handed it to me.

I felt heat on my face. We were at a romantic table, in a romantic restaurant and now he was handing me a gift? I gulped, feeling under pressure. I opened the envelope and inside was a card with the Millar's Hotel logo on it.

"It's for a spa day. I've spoken to both Izzy and Annie and they have booked tomorrow off work so the three of you can enjoy time together."

I felt a lump in my throat. "That's so sweet."

That was the thing with H. He wound me up no end to the point where I wanted to shout at him to get off my case, to leave me alone, then he'd do something like this.

"Thank you." I put the card in my bag. "I could really do with some relaxation."

"You deserve it." H's phone lit up on the table. "Sorry, Becky, I have to get this." He leaned back in his seat and looked out of the window.

I decided that it would be a good time for me to go to the ladies.

Having touched up my make-up, I put some extra powder on my face. It appeared flushed, which I guessed was from the wine. The door swung open. It was Elena.

"Hi," I said.

She blinked, her eyes were red.

"Are you okay?"

She nodded. "Yes, sorry. I am sentimental. Tonight, I was supposed to be at the theatre, with a friend who has died."

"Robert?"

She nodded. "I recognise you from the funeral. If he killed himself, it was all my fault. We had a disagreement before he was found. But you think it was murder?"

I nodded. "And so do the police. I'm sure he loved you very much."

She pulled a tissue from a box and gave a small sob.

I approached her but she took a step backwards and shook her head. "I must be composed."

I opened my mouth to question her further but my instinct told me all I needed to know. It wasn't her.

"I hope you enjoy your meal." She left the room.

When I exited the restroom, H was still on the phone. I didn't want to intrude on his conversation, so studied a large picture, hung on the wall, of Branden Bay in the Victorian times. The women wore hats and long dresses and bathing carts dotted the beach. I glanced over to see if H was off the phone yet and behind him out of the window, I spotted a woman, walking down the High Street. *Is that Dannie?* I thought. I knew H would be mad at me, but I could not let her get away. I needed to know what she was after in that box of things at Chesham's. I had questions to ask her. I slipped out of the restaurant. I ran in an effort to catch her up.

"Dannie," I called her name. She didn't turn around so I started to jog after her.

"Becky," I heard H bellow from behind. *That's all I need,* I thought and stopped as he sprinted up to me.

"What are you doing? I thought we were having a nice evening?"

"I think I just saw Dannie from Chesham's."

"Where?"

I turned back to the street. "She's gone now." I put my hands on my hips. "I've lost her. Well done, H"

He shook his head. "Couldn't you just let us have one nice evening together? To explore the connection?"

"What connection? The one between Robert and Nick Pope?"

"No." He shook his head and ran a hand through his hair. "Don't you ever think there might be a reason everyone assumes we're a couple? Do you know what I'm saying?"

"Not really." I sighed. I was having a hard time trying to figure out who killed Robert, I had no time for extra riddles. I was mad at him for letting Dannie slip away like that. "All you ever do is criticise me. Telling me what to do, what not to do. You ... you ... stand there with all your muscles." *What did I say that for?* I asked myself.

He shook his head. "Are you surprised? You won't listen to any sense – you think you know it all and you don't. You think you can be a private detective but what training do you have? None. I've spent seven years in the force and I'm still learning. I'm telling you, all your problems are your own fault. If you'd listened to other people and kept away from Nick Pope, you wouldn't be in this mess."

I stepped back. "As I said, you're constantly criticising me and putting me down."

He took a deep breath. "I … I just …"

I rearranged by bag on my shoulder. "I think it's time to go home. Don't you? And by home I mean I'll go to my house and you go to yours."

"But …" he called after me.

I swung around. "No, H. I need to be alone. Respect my privacy, even if you don't respect me as a person." I stormed down the High Street. I felt bad, leaving him to go back to Corelli's alone and pick up the bill – but I was shaking with rage. How could he cause a scene when I had so much stress in my life?

As I pulled back my curtains the following morning, Constance jumped onto the windowsill. I'd woken to a text from H asking if I was okay and wishing me a good day at Millar's. As I watched the postman walking up Beach Road delivering letters, I wondered whether Carol had suggested H take me out. She probably picked up the voucher from Millar's as well. When I was with my ex, Marcus, his secretary used to buy my presents – I guessed it was a guy thing. I was glad it was a sunny day because I would have to leave Constance in the garden while I was out because I'd not invested in a litter tray.

I opened my bag to prepare for Millar's and turned to pick up my swim suit to find Constance had jumped into my tote. "No, you can't come with me. I'm going to the spa," I said waggling my finger at her.

She meowed as I put her out in the back garden. She was safer there than at the front of the house and she could always jump the wall and pester Lynn for treats. As I left, I glanced at the closed café doors and felt tears prick my eyes. I prayed that my troubles would soon be over so I could get back to the life I wanted.

I met Annie at the corner of the High Street and gave her a hug. She slipped an arm into mine and we continued our journey towards the hotel.

"I miss you so much. I'm sorry I've been stuck at work," she said. "I had to be really assertive yesterday when I asked for today off."

"Are they having extra visitors?"

"No, I've been promoted."

"Congratulations." I smiled at Annie but her mouth was downcast. "Why are you looking sad. That's a good thing isn't it?"

Annie sighed. "It would be, but I'm the only long-standing member of staff left. So they didn't have much to choose from. But I don't want to talk about that right now." She squeezed my arm. "What I want to know is, how did the big date go last night, eh?"

"Date?"

"Yes, H? The romantic table for two at Corelli's?"

"That wasn't a date. He just wanted to get out of the house. And no, it didn't go well he used it as yet another opportunity to put me down."

"Like what?"

"I don't want to talk about it." I sighed. "I'm looking forward to a day of pampering before I'm thrown in the slammer."

"Don't say that."

"Rachael said the DNA results are expected later today. With my hair found on a dead body, I'm bound to be arrested."

"Rachael's an excellent lawyer, I'm sure she'll get you bail."

As we reached Millar's, Izzy was inside the entrance waiting. "Oh, there you are, my darlings." She raised her left eyebrow. "So, sweetie. How did your hot date go last night?"

"Why does everyone think I went on a date? It was just dinner with H."

Annie looked at Izzy and shrugged her shoulders. "Well, come on then, seeing as H went to the trouble to get us these tickets – let's get inside."

We walked towards the spa entrance. As soon as the door opened, I was met by the evocative aromas of eucalyptus and rosemary, which instantly calmed me. I was determined to enjoy the day.

We had a stress-free couple of hours, discussing

things other than the case. After trying out the various steam rooms and the sauna, we lay in the meditation room, listening to eastern music as aromatherapy snaked through the air. But try as I might to meditate, every time I shut my eyes, I saw pictures relating to the murders. Visions of Robert floated across my mind with his face practically falling off. Of a faceless dancer with long blonde hair at the Fantasy Lounge. Of Mia cutting my hair out at Millar's and paying a hit woman with stolen money. Of Dannie scowling at me at Chesham's reception. Of Sarah helping me dish out poisoned cakes to the staff and of Elena pushing Robert off a cliff. After all, it could have been any one of them and was I a good enough judge of character to be able to fully eliminate any of them?

It was soon lunch and I welcomed it. Being alone with my thoughts was not proving to be the getting-away-from-it-all experience I'd hoped it would be.

As we left the meditation room, Annie's skin shone with a golden glow, Izzy's beamed youthfully pink and mine, no doubt, was steaming red, clashing horribly with my hair.

"You look like you have the world on your shoulders, darling," said Izzy cocking her head to one side. She slipped a long arm over my shoulders. "Let's eat. That will take your mind off things."

We walked towards the small spa restaurant, which was decorated to resemble a roman garden with white walls and pillars, and green leafed plants in every available space.

I sighed. “My mind’s on overdrive.”

Annie rubbed my back, as she followed. “It’ll be all right in the end – I’m sure.”

We took a seat next to a pillar with vines growing up it.

Annie sat down. “H will fight for you. He’s been working so hard to clear your name”

“Has he?”

“Yes, he was up here for hours yesterday, trying to figure out who put that chewing gum in your hair.”

“He did?”

“Yes, darling,” said Izzy. “That’s how he wangled these passes for us. He bought them in exchange for an off the record peek at the CCTV”

Annie laughed. “H plays by the rules but he bends them when he has to.” She put a hand on mine “He’s really cut up about having to take you into the police station the other day. He wants to make everything right for you. And he’s got contacts in Bristol who are getting hold of CCTV for him, of the streets around the Fantasy Lounge. With that detective inspector thinking you’re the killer, they haven’t been following any other lines of enquiry so H is doing all he can to get evidence and get you off the hook.”

“Why didn’t he tell me that last night?” I said. Although, had I given him enough time to? I was so busy chasing Dannie up the road.

"He's looking out for you, sweetie." Izzy smiled.

I felt a pang of guilt and rubbed the front of my neck. I'd maybe misread H the night before. I decided to text him as soon as I retrieved my phone from the changing rooms, to thank him for the spa day and for all he was doing for me.

Annie picked up a newspaper which the previous occupant of the table must have left behind. "Cryptic crosswords, I love these. There are a few still to do."

"Not my scene, darling." Izzy picked up the lunch menu.

I did the same. Although nothing I deemed comfort food was on offer.

Annie held the newspaper up. "What about this one? 'They see' and the answer is a three-letter word followed by a four-letter word."

I thought about it for a few seconds. "Ah, the eyes," I said smiling, I loved solving puzzles. "It's an anagram." I heard the words echo around my head.

Annie raised her eyebrows. "Wow – you're good at this."

"Oh my goodness," I said.

Izzy put a hand on my arm. "Are you okay, darling?"

"It's an anagram."

"Yes," Izzy said slowly. "You already said, sweetie. Now what are you having to eat?"

"Nadine."

Annie put the paper down. "You're talking about the case. Remember – it's off limits."

"Dannie and Nadine." My voice had reached a high pitch and I was drawing attention from neighbouring tables.

Annie placed a hand on mine. "Try to remain calm."

"But Dannie and Nadine are the same person."

CHAPTER 19

Izzy dropped the menu. "O-M-G, darling you're amazing."

"Hey, we're supposed to be taking time out here. Not discussing murders," whispered Annie.

"I need to find her." I stood up.

"No," said Annie. "You need to rest and store up your energy."

"At least let me speak to H?" I placed my palms on the table. "I don't know where Dannie is – she could have left town." I also needed to break the ice with him. I felt a tad guilty at how I had shouted at him the night before. "This lead could get me off. Don't forget the DNA is expected back today and you know they'll have a match for my hair."

"Okay – one call to H and that's it. I'll order your lunch."

After fetching my phone from the locker, I made

the call in the changing rooms which were empty. H answered straight away.

"I'm glad you called," H said. "Are you finding the spa relaxing?"

"I have some information for you."

H made no comment.

I continued. "It's Dannie, the receptionist from Robert's office, she's the dancer from The Fantasy Lounge."

"How have you come to that conclusion?"

"Nadine is an anagram of Dannie. Nadine is her stripper name – literally."

"You haven't made contact with her, have you?"

"No. Look, they're both blonde, and she's the connection – someone who knew both Robert Hart and Nick Pope. And the barman said that Nadine left with a suit. I'm guessing that was Robert. Apparently, Dannie turned up at Chesham's one day after Robert had given her a job without a formal interview. She could have been the one to steal Nick Pope's money, having access to the computer system. In fact, she said she'd studied accountancy at Uni, she's probably a mastermind thief. And she could have easily gone to the club – telling Nick she had his money or something. Went out the back with him and stabbed him."

"Hey. Slow down. I'll get a pen to get this on paper."

I waited a few seconds. It all seemed to fit into place. Robert led me to the offices – she was the first person I met. He pointed to the side of the church she was sitting in. She obviously was the one that stole the money too. No-one at Chesham's seemed to know her that well. Who really knew her background?

"Right I'm back," said H. "What else?"

"The day after Nick Pope's murder, Dannie was late to work and given the sack because she was rummaging around a box in his office and inside was a knife."

"A knife?"

"Yes, one of those red one's with different blades. A Swiss army knife."

"The post mortem showed, Pope died from multiple wounds from a short blade. But why would she be putting the knife in that box? Surely she would have thrown it off the cliff?"

"It's the ideal hiding place. Don't you see? Who's going to look in Robert Hart's possessions for the weapon used in a murder after his death? It's the perfect place to hide it."

"I'll get them to collect the box."

"No need. Chesham's had a request to return the box to the police."

"How do you know all of this?"

"I was there. Check it for her prints. It's got to be her. And when Mia cut the chewing gum out of my hair - Dannie was in a cubicle. She probably bought a red wig and set off to Nick's place that night with the strands of my hair."

H paused for a couple of seconds. "If I tip Brad off,

they pull her in. If it's not her, my job could be on the line. They told me to keep away."

"If you don't bring her in, I'm going to look for her myself."

"Okay. I'll call it in. And Becky, stay put at Millar's and don't go anywhere until I get there. I'll probably be a few hours."

My hands shook as I ended the call and placed the phone in my robe pocket.

Back at the table I picked at the salad which Izzy had ordered for me. It had odd looking shoots in it, shavings of beetroot and various types of lettuce leaves sprinkled with nuts. It wasn't a proper lunch – it looked more like a side dish.

Izzy broke the silence. "From what I remember of her from the funeral, Dannie was not much more than a girl. It's hard to imagine her as a killer. And to handle Nick Pope?"

"She has a temper on her, though," I said. "She might be working with someone else. And if she was giving Nick a massage or er ... something. He might not have been paying too much attention when she stabbed him."

Annie stood up. "I'm ready for the roof top hot tub. Let's take our glasses of bubbly up there." She glanced at me. "You need to calm down." She was right – after all, if the police could not get a confession out of Dannie, this could be my last few hours of freedom. I had to enjoy them.

We spent a good hour and a half on the roof top. I hoped the police had pulled Dannie in. I lay back. The fizz of champagne and bubbles of the hot tub, relaxed me as I looked across the sandy bay, through the Perspex barrier which stopped the wind but retained the view. I lived in such a beautiful town, I wished I could relax and enjoy it.

"You look so much better now, Becky. Let's go for our treatments," Annie said.

Annie was booked in for a mud bath, Izzy was trying out the floatation tank and I was lined up for a stress relieving facial.

"And give me your phone." Annie stuck her hand out as I put my robe back on.

"But H might call."

"Do as she says, darling. You need total relaxation."

I sighed as I handed it over and watched Annie slip it into her robe pocket.

In the treatment room, I lay back on the bed, which was covered in warm towels. As the beautician cleansed my skin, it felt amazing, as if my body was melting into the soft bed. Once my skin had been cleansed the beautician applied a thick layer of chilled green gunk to my face. She spoke in a slow low breathy voice. "This will bring out any remaining toxins before I give you a hands-on facial massage with a specially formulated rub, fortified with vitamins and nutrients to make your skin zing."

I wasn't convinced about the skin zinging part; I knew what my face looked like after too much fuss. I just hoped that H could wrap the case up soon, because I wouldn't want to be dragged into the police station tomorrow with a face covered in post face-pack pimples. I hadn't thought that through when I booked the treatment. But hey, I had loads on my mind.

"I'll leave you for fifteen minutes to let the face pack do its magic, before I give you a head massage."

I lay still for what seemed like an eternity, but was probably only five minutes. Being alone, I could not escape my thoughts and I found myself fighting the urge to go to the ladies room. The music playing in the background emitted the sounds of a zen garden, with a running water feature. Annie had been urging me all day to drink water to flush out my system. Then she made me down another half pint, to counteract the two glasses of fizz. I sat up on the bed and the beautician popped her head around the door.

"Everything okay in here?"

"I need to use the toilet"

"Okay. Keep your chin up to keep the pack in place and be as quick as you can, otherwise it will melt," she said smiling but I sensed she was none too pleased.

I decided to use the disabled toilet – it was a lot more private. I was as quick as possible and as I came out of the small room, I heard a familiar voice from the spa reception.

"Ha ha, silly me," said Sarah, signing out. Her chin-length hair had been blow dried into a smooth sleek style with caramel highlights. She turned and I waved at her. Frowning, she stared back at me. It was then that I remembered I was wearing a face mask of green gunk, which was dripping off my chin onto the white fluffy towelling robe. I really needed to lay down but I wanted to ask her about Dannie. About whether she had been in touch with her. If she knew where she was living. It would help if the police had trouble tracking her down.

I approached Sarah as she placed the pen back on top of the signing-out book.

"Sarah. It's me, Becky."

She smiled. "So it is."

"I wanted to ask you about Dannie. Have you seen her?"

She shook her head. "No, thank goodness."

"Oh, okay. Do you know where she lives?"

"I'm afraid not. We weren't that close."

I felt my shoulders droop. Without Dannie it was unlikely I would shrug off the tag 'prime suspect' as far as Bad Cop Brad was concerned.

"Why?" she asked, as she lifted her arm to touch her perfectly groomed hair. As she did, I noticed four scratches down her arm.

"That looks nasty," I said.

"I got caught in some brambles this morning, while gardening for an old lady who lives up the road from me. I'm in a rush right now, but I'll ask around to see if anyone has heard from Dannie. Although it's unlikely. She wasn't exactly popular in the office." She disappeared with a wave.

I tutted – something nagged at me as I watched her walk away.

The receptionist sighed. "Lucky girl. Off on holiday."

"Nice," I said. I glanced down at the book where Sarah had signed out. I frowned – there was a crossed-out signature next to her name.

"She's had quite a makeover that one. Came in a couple of weeks ago, split up with someone she'd said, cut her hair off. Seems an odd thing to do to me – but it's common." She ran her hand down her own extra-long locks tied back in a pony tail.

I blinked at her. "What did you say?"

"People cut their hair when they have their heart broken. I'd never do that."

"She had long hair?"

"Yeah long and scraggy. No offence but she was a bit dull. Now look at her. New nails, shaped eyebrows." She lowered her voice. "Botox and a bit of cheek filler. She's spent a fortune in here these past couple of weeks. They must pay pretty well up at Chesham's, that's all I can say." She took a deep breath. "Did you see those shoes she was wearing?

She wouldn't have had much change from five hundred."

I stared down at the signature. Crossed out was the name 'Robert Hart' written in elaborate hand, then beside that Sarah Stone.

The receptionist laughed. "Said she was so used to signing everything for her boss, she keeps signing his name instead of her own." She put her head to one side. "Shame he killed himself though, innit?"

My mouth fell open as a blob of face pack landed on the visitors' book. "Sorry," I said staring down at the sheet. "I need this." I tore the page out of the book.

"What d'ya think you're doing?" she asked.

I looked at the door. I had to follow Sarah. I didn't have time to drag Annie out of her mud bath to get my mobile phone. I had to go after her now – to be sure.

I bolted for the door.

"Hey, come back with that," shouted the receptionist.

Outside, I saw Sarah about fifty yards away, walking towards the sea front. "Sarah," I called, but she was too far away to hear. I felt self-conscious as people stared at me. I was after all, barefoot in a white robe – or should I say a white robe with green splatters. I ran down the sloping street, gaining on her. "Sarah."

She stopped and looked at me. As I got closer our eyes met and hers narrowed. Retrieving a mobile phone from her pocket she made a call as she continued her journey, at a brisk pace.

"Stop," I shouted as I followed. I broke into a sprint, well a jog. My feet went as fast as they could, considering the rough state of the pavement beneath them. My robe flapped open and I re-tied it, I only had a swim suit underneath. I reached the seafront and looked around. Feeling a buzz of sharp electricity, to my left I saw the familiar shape of Robert, lolloping along the road, his face practically oozing off his head – a bit like my face pack.

"Where is she?" I shouted at him. A nearby deckchair attendant looked at me as if I was mad, talking to thin air. Robert lifted his hand as if to point and then his arm fell off.

"Urgh!" I looked to the left and then the right until I spotted her and broke into another run. My poor spa softened soles felt sore, as they pounded the pavement. Once on the prom, I held onto the back of a bench to catch my breath. A little girl walked past with her mother.

"Can I borrow your phone?" I held out a sloppy green hand.

"Mummy, what's wrong with that lady?"

"Don't look, honey. Hurry along."

I shut my eyes. My feet felt as if they'd been rubbed with a course sandpaper. Sarah was nowhere in sight. I'd have to return to Millar's and get dressed. It dawned on me, I'd probably got poor Dannie arrested, I was now sure she was in fact innocent. And I was going to be in so much trouble with H. I heard the sound of police sirens, assuming they were probably on their way now to pick Dannie up.

I turned back in the direction of Hill road, to get back to Millar's. I heard someone call my name. I looked up the prom as a drip of face pack blurred my vision, I wiped it to see H running towards me.

The sirens became louder and a police car rounded the corner, heading right for me. I looked around to see if I could figure out what the emergency was, but no-one was behind me. Speeding down Hill Road was a black four-wheel drive. It screeched onto the end of the prom and stopped just a few feet from me. Out jumped Bad Cop Brad.

CHAPTER 20

As I stood at the end of the prom, surrounded by police officers and a growing crowd of passers-by, H reached my side.

He bent over to catch his breath. "The DNA test has come through, confirming your hair was found on Nick's body."

"What about Dannie?"

"That's what we'd like to know," said Bad Cop, DCI Brad Harris as he reached me. "Thought you were clever, did you? Covering up your crime by framing someone else? We've just released Miss Danielle Strickland."

"Oh no. The poor girl." I put a hand to my cheek then regretted it as I felt the remaining green gloop. I wiped my hand, onto the robe.

"A top tip for you, Miss James – if you ever see freedom again, that is. The first thing you do with a suspect is to check where they were at the time of the murder, or murders in this case. Dannielle Strickland had rock solid alibis for both killings. Unlike you."

"It's not Dannie, it's Sarah Stone. Robert's PA that killed him."

Brad shook his head. "Give up on the lies, Miss James. We have DNA to place you at the scene of the murder of Nick Pope and now we have the murder weapon found on your property, covered in your fingerprints."

"What?"

"A red Swiss army knife, found in an empty paint pot in your garden shed. Good hiding place but not good enough."

H turned to me. "You handled the knife when you saw it at Chesham's?"

Oh dear, I thought. I was so focussed on the murderer's prints possibly being on the knife I clean forgot that the last set of prints on there would be mine. H was right, I did have a lot to learn. "Sarah tricked me into touching the knife at Chesham's. She got me up to the office on the pretence of delivering cakes and must have planted the knife in my shed." I guessed she'd totally made up the bit about Dannie rummaging through the box. Sarah probably took it out before the box was sent back to the police station. "And how did you know I was here? She obviously tipped you off about ten minutes ago."

"Enough." Brad stepped forward. "Rebecca James I'm arresting you –"

"Not this again." I stepped back.

"Let's listen to what Becky has to say," said H. "I know she hasn't done it."

Brad took a deep breath and placed a hand on my arm. "For the murders of Nicolas Pope and Robert Hart."

"H please tell him to stop."

Brad turned to H. "Mate, you need to back off. You're letting your heart rule your head. This girl's a nightmare. Go home and let me finish this off."

"Please H, you can't let them take me like this." I pulled my arm away from Brad's rough grip.

Brad continued as he grabbed my arm again. "You do not have to say anything, but it may harm your defence if you do not mention, when questioned, something which you later rely on in court."

"No. I can't go like this?" I threw my free arm in the air. "I need to change and wash my face. I'm not even wearing shoes."

"Look Brad, at least let her put some clothes on," said H.

Brad growled. "It's DCI Harris when I'm on duty. You've got fifteen minutes and I'll have a car waiting outside her house. We'll take her in – not you. And forensics will be going over her house."

"Thanks, gov," H said.

I felt metal around my left wrist. "You're cuffing

me?" I looked over my shoulder to H as he clipped the other cuff onto his right hand. A group of spectators was forming and I put my head down.

H walked with me towards my house, which was only two hundred yards away, as tears of sheer anger mixed into what was left of the face pack.

"I'm putting my job on the line for you here." He didn't sound pleased with me. "And I told you to stay at Millar's. You never listen."

"I had to follow her. It's definitely Sarah. She must have planted the knife in my shed."

"To get you off we need to focus on eliminating the evidence they have on you. By accusing two other people in the space of a few hours – all you have achieved is to make yourself look guilty. You need to trust me and keep quiet. Let Rachael do the talking."

As we walked along the prom, a convoy of three police cars and Brad's black four-wheel drive followed. Once outside my house, H unlocked the front door.

Entering, I looked around for my cat. What I needed was a cuddle with my fluffy companion, but she was nowhere to be seen. I called her three times before I remembered I'd left her in the garden.

"Forget the cat, you need to clean up and change into something smart. They may put you in court as soon as there is an available slot. I'll ask Rachael to meet us at the station."

I lifted my arm. "You need to uncuff me. I need privacy to get ready."

"Okay, but be quick," he said as he released me.

Upstairs, I washed my face with cold water. After patting it dry with a towel, I checked it out in the mirror. My skin was blotchy but I had no time for make-up. I put on a suit and a pair of flat shoes. I couldn't wear stilettos as my feet were killing me. Peering through the curtains, I saw the police car and Brad's black four by four.

As I came down the stairs, I could hear H speaking on the phone. "Thanks, Rachael, I'll make that crystal clear to her. But whether she takes heed or not ..."

I reckon I've a couple of minutes, I thought, *to find Constance.*

I rushed to the snug, opening the French doors to the garden, I called Constance. A growing dread crept across my chest. It wasn't right – Constance always run up when I called her name.

"Constance, Connie Cat." I called quietly into the garden. The silence felt menacing. I saw a flash of blue, out of the corner of my vision accompanied by a burst of static. "Grandma?" I called and rubbed my eyes, I was sure I'd seen her, wearing an aqua dress, her wavy red hair flowing onto her shoulders. She'd been standing beside the apple tree. But now she was gone. As I approached the spot where I'd seen her, I noticed a ball of fluff laying in the grass. I rushed over until I reached my cat and put a shaking hand onto her small body.

I gasped. "Connie."

My eyes smarted with tears as I picked up her limp body. I cried out. "No." There was a red gash on her stomach.

The back gate swung open and Lynn appeared. "Lovey, what's going on? I had a feeling something wasn't right, then heard your voice."

I opened my mouth but could no longer speak. Lifting my arms, I showed Lynn my limp cat.

"I'll call Jeff to take us to the vet, follow me I'll get a towel. The poor little mite."

I followed, cradling the cat I loved, realising I was getting blood on my suit, but I didn't care about that, all I cared about was my beautiful pet. The gate clanged shut behind us. Jeff was there within a few minutes, he'd been on the road when Lynn called.

"Go straight to the animal hospital in Branden Way," she said to Jeff as we climbed in.

I blinked. Tears stung my eyes as we sat in the front three seats of the van.

"You look smart where were you off to?" asked Jeff

Oh dear, I thought. "Actually, I'm under arrest and supposed to be going to the police station."

"What?" asked Lynn.

I shook my head. "H is going to kill me."

"Tell us about it," Jeff said.

So I did. And then when I got to the bit where I'd seen Sarah in reception, I remembered the scratches on her arm. "She stabbed Connie. Brave Constance must have attacked Sarah while she was planting the knife in my shed. And now Sarah's probably on a plane somewhere and no one will find her."

Once we arrived at the animal hospital, the staff were fantastic.

"She's still alive. Has she been in an accident?" A nurse asked.

"I think someone stabbed her," I choked on my tears.

They checked the wound. "We'll do a scan; it won't be cheap but we need to make sure there's no damage to vital organs before we stitch her up."

"I'll wait with Constance, lovey," said Lynn then turned to Jeff. "You'll have to drop Becky at the police station, otherwise she'll be in even more bother. Take her straight there."

I sighed, knowing Lynn was right. If I didn't get down there quick, I'd be seen as a fugitive.

I climbed into the van after being assured by Lynn that she would text Jeff when there was news about Constance. Tears streamed down my face as we drove back into the town. As we reached the High Street, I saw a woman pulling a suit case towards the bus stop. It was Sarah.

"Stop," I shouted slapping my hand on the dash. Jeff slammed on the brakes.

I unclipped my seat belt and wiped the tears off my face. I had to be strong.

"What are you doing?" Jeff asked.

I jumped out. "It's Sarah. Call H and tell him where I am."

"Becky, let me come with you."

I turned around and shook my head. "Just call him."

I hurried down the road. Sarah headed for the prom bus stop where the shuttle picked up passengers to take them to Bristol Airport.

Oh no you don't, I thought as I caught up with her. She reached the prom and retracted the handle of her case. "You're in so much trouble," I said.

She turned and raised her eyebrows. "Me? I'm not the one who's face is all over the TV and internet. Branden Bay's most wanted."

Oh no, I thought.

"Your mugshot's everywhere. Seems you gave the police the slip."

I heard the blades of a helicopter in the distance.

"Everyone's looking for you." She grinned at me. Nice, safe Sarah had turned into a menacing psychopath.

"You know I'm innocent. We both know who killed Robert." I put my hands on my hips in an effort to stop my arms shaking. "So why did you do it?" I turned my back on Sarah to see if I could still see Jeff's van. It was gone, maybe he was parking up. I felt something pressed into my back.

"Don't do anything silly Becky. Or this knife in my hand may slip. Let's take a walk to the jetty," Sarah said, leaving her case at the bus stop as she led me across the promenade.

"Is this what you did to Robert?" I asked. I wanted a confession from her, even if it was the last thing I heard before I died.

"He was an idiot. He could have had a new life with me in Thailand. I knew his marriage was a farce and he worked so hard. I found a way he could be free; we could both live in paradise."

"So you stole Nick's money?" I said as we neared the jetty.

"It was hardly Nick's money – he made it off other people's hard work and drugs. I covered my tracks – it would have been ages before they realised I'd taken it. They'd never have caught up with us. I thought Robert would be pleased. It was his way out. He could get away and we could have a simple life together. I'd loved him for so long and confessed my true feelings to him. But he went ballistic. How was I supposed to know Nick had asked him to make a huge withdrawal?"

"You could have just given it back? Why did you have to kill Robert?"

"I didn't mean to. He asked me to meet him after dark, on the prom, to discuss it. I thought he might have changed his mind, but no, he said I had to give the money back, or he would report me. I told him it was dirty money and Nick would never have told the police. I'd worked hard to syphon off that cash and said I would go to Thailand without him if he wouldn't join me." She shook her head. "He stormed off, saying he would be telling Graham. I followed him here." She stopped as we reached the start of the jetty. "I pleaded with him to take a chance on love. He called me crazy, said he could never love me and that he was in love with that Italian woman from the wine bar. I lost my temper and he looked at me as if I was mad. He stepped back a few paces onto the jetty and I pushed him in anger. How was I to know Robert couldn't swim? No-one was around. It was high tide. I watched him flounder and then he was gone. Washed away with the tide I guess." She slackened her grip. "It was so peaceful afterwards, I sat here for a while, remembering the good times."

I yanked my arm back, but Sarah retained her grip.

"Nice try." She led me down the jetty.

"And why have you got a knife on you anyway? You'd never be able to take it on the plane."

"In case I needed it in self-defence. After all, I heard there was an assassin on the loose." She laughed in a most evil way as she pushed me along the wooden boards. "So, tell me – how did you know it was me?"

"Your signature," I said. "You signed Robert's name in the book at Millar's. I realised you could easily have signed the suicide note and then when the graphologist asked for an example of Robert's handwriting to check against it, you probably provided them with something else you'd already signed on his behalf."

"Very clever. It's a shame, because I was simply going to hand you over to the police, now they have the murder weapon with your finger prints on. You're so easy and so obvious. You walked straight into that one. I put the knife in the box the morning after I'd used it on that pig Pope." She laughed. "Killing him was as easy as stealing from him. The disgusting creep."

"Why kill him?"

"He'd put a call through to Graham, asking for the withdrawal of his money. I couldn't risk Chesham's finding out that most of it was missing, before I'd got the plane out of here." Sarah pushed me along the last few yards of the jetty. "So, Pope had to die. I thought why not frame you? All I needed was some of your hair and that part was easy. I was going to offer to cut the chewing gum out myself, but Mia took over and unwittingly made my life a lot simpler. It was perfect."

"They'll find out it's you that took Nick's money."

"Nick's dead. He can't tell them it was stolen, so no-one's looking for it."

"I hate to be the bearer of bad news but the police know that Robert and Nick's deaths are connected. You'll never get out of the country."

"The evidence points to you and you won't be around to defend yourself."

I felt her pull her elbow out. *She's going to stab me!* I screamed in my head.

"Leave her alone." Jeff ran towards us.

Sarah lurched at me and I stepped to one side, just missing the blade.

"Stop," I heard a deep voice, as H thundered down the planks.

Sarah looked over at them then back to me. She lifted the knife.

Now I may not have been educated in self-defence but I was trained in ballet. I lifted my leg and kicked the knife out of her hand. "And you stabbed my cat," I shouted as I lunged towards her in a much less ladylike manner. H pulled me back.

Police sirens filled my ears and passers-by pointed, screamed and shouted a repeated phrase: 'The Medium Assassin'. I really had been plastered over the TV.

"Are you okay?" H held me by the shoulders and then turned to the approaching officers. "Arrest that woman," he said pointing to Sarah as she lay on the boards of the jetty.

As the officers picked her up, she screamed. "Let go of me."

"It's thanks to Jeff that you're still alive," said H.

Jeff's face was crimson. "Are you okay?"

I nodded. "How's Constance?"

"She's conscious and is going to pull through."

I felt a big fat tear of relief run down my cheek.

H led me to the waiting police cars. "Forensic accounting located three hundred thousand which had originated with Nick Pope, passed through Chesham's and is now sitting in various accounts in Switzerland in the name of a Sarah Stone."

"Thank goodness for that."

"But it's going to be a long night and you could still be charged with wasting police time after you gave us the slip."

Brad stood with his arms crossed. leaning against his car with an expression as dark as his transport's paintwork.

CHAPTER 21

I don't think I've ever been as tired as I was when I walked into Branden Bay Animal Hospital at half eight in the morning. Annie had brought me straight from the police station after I'd endured hours of grilling by DCI Brad Harris. He knew it wasn't me who killed Robert or Nick, but he still treated me like a criminal – my punishment I guess for getting in the way of his case, although Rachael told me she didn't think they would pursue the 'wasting police time' stance. He had warned me that he never expected to see me interfering in one of his cases again.

Happiness surged through me for the first time in weeks.

"Come this way, Miss James," the nurse led me to the consulting room.

My bottom lip trembled as soon as I saw my cat,

sitting on the table with a huge cone shaped collar around her neck, turning her nose up at a bowl.

"We want her to eat before we release her, but she's refusing food."

"She prefers poached salmon."

At the sound of my voice Constance looked up, giving a whimpering meow. The tears spilled down my cheeks.

Annie rubbed my back. "She's a strong one."

"We've given her an antibiotic injection and a strong pain killer," said the nurse.

I placed the pet carrier I had bought for her on the table next to her. It was made of canvass with a window in it. I couldn't have turned up at the animal hospital to collect her with a designer tote. As soon as I opened the flap, Constance shuffled inside without complaining. "Come on, Connie I'll make you your favourite food when we get home."

Jeff was waiting for us outside my house.

"Thanks again, Jeff, for yesterday"

"Just doing my job. As your gatekeeper."

I laughed. I didn't think for one moment that Jeff was this so-called gatekeeper, but whether it was a thing or not, he'd certainly been there for me.

Jeff had to get off to work, but Annie came inside with me. My chest felt warm as I looked at the café doors, knowing that tomorrow I would be reopening and getting on with my life.

Once inside, I found Lynn in my kitchen, making

up bowls of sponge mix, with Grandma's battered recipe book at her side. I'd asked her for help as I needed to bake a fair few cakes if I was to open the following day.

"I'll give you a hand," said Annie as she approached Lynn.

Izzy sat at the kitchen table, chatting on the phone and scribbling away. "Great timing." She handed me her mobile. "Mia wants a word."

I took the phone. "I'm so sorry I've not been in touch, Mia. I wasn't able to because I was your supposed paid assassin."

"Don't worry, my lawyer spoke to your lawyer. Thanks so much for everything you've done. I'd never have suspected Sarah."

"I'm guessing she had a fixation with Robert," I said. "Which I'm sure was not reciprocated."

"I've had a lot of time alone to think while in the cell and have come to accept that our marriage only existed in name. Things hadn't been right for ages. We should have split up. But it was easy with me in Devon and him up there in Branden Bay. Neither of us could face the stress of a divorce."

"You can start again," I said.

"True and you've been a real inspiration to me, Becky, with what you've done making a new life for yourself in a different town. I've decided it's time I made something of myself too. I want a career."

"Good luck."

"And what of Robert? Was he involved? Did you use your psychic powers?"

I hesitated. I didn't really want to tell Mia that he'd been slowly turning into some sort of melting zombie before my eyes. But, watching Izzy reading her notes, I knew it would soon be in the newspaper. So I told her, but reiterated, that what I saw was just my third eye interpreting the spiritual world. He wasn't actually a zombie. "I'm sure he'll rest in peace knowing his killer is behind bars."

I heard Constance meowing from the bag. "I've got someone here who needs feeding." I said farewell and passed the phone back to Izzy.

"The salmon steak is in the fridge," said Lynn. "I'll pop this cake in the oven. Get yourselves into the snug, and I'll bring drinks in and get that poor little mite's breakfast on."

As we drank tea, Constance sat on my lap as I fed her flakes of fish because she found it difficult to reach it with the cone around her neck. Izzy, Lynn and Annie chatted away, praising me and laughing as they asked me again to tell them about my pole dancing attempt at the Fantasy Lounge.

The world began to look good again, but there were a couple of things troubling me. Two people I felt I owed an apology, firstly Dannie and secondly H.

. . .

THE FOLLOWING DAY, THE CAFE BUZZED WITH customers, all looking at me as if I was a celeb. *My days of going undercover in Branden Bay are well and truly over,* I thought. I had no intention of investigating anything ever again, especially as the award-winning cop, DCI Brad Harris had told me he would arrest me on the spot if he saw me anywhere near a police investigation.

I was in the kitchen making up sandwiches when I heard a knock at the door. It was Dannie.

"The lady in the café said I could come back here to see you?"

I'd left my number at Chesham's and asked them to pass on my apologies to Dannie and said that I hoped we could meet so that I could say sorry in person. I have to say, I was surprised that she'd shown up. "Come through," I said, washing my hands under the tap. "Do you want a drink or cake?"

"No, I'm fine. I got a message you wanted to see me?" Dannie looked weary for someone so young.

I took her into the snug and motioned for her to sit down. "I'm so sorry I put you in the frame. Sarah had said you were rummaging in a box at Chesham's. I realise now she made it up and was leading me up the garden path."

Dannie shook her head. "I knew someone was out to get me. Since Robert died, I'd been accused of all sorts of things around the office – which led to them asking me to leave. I probably didn't do myself any favours when I told Graham where to stick his job."

"Can you go back now? They must know Sarah was behind your sacking?"

"Word's got out now - about my dancing at Nicks. They'll all be talking about me."

"Sorry about that. I've made it quite clear to my friend at the Gazette that your name should not be mentioned anywhere in her report."

Danny looked me straight in the eye. "I wasn't proud of my dancing. But that's all it was. I didn't do anything else."

"Look, I'm not judging you."

"And I only worked there for a few nights until Robert ..."

"So you had an affair with him?"

She scrunched her petite nose. "No way. He was like an uncle to me. He and my father went to University together." She shook her head. "He was there to see Nick about business and saw me dancing. I'm not sure what went on between them but I knew Nick was piling pressure on him to do something he didn't want to."

"I guess it's wrong to speak ill of the dead, but I'm gathering Nick was corrupt."

"He was a bully. Robert was totally shocked when he saw me at the club. I was so embarrassed. He threatened to tell my parents unless I moved from Bristol to Branden Bay and took a job as a receptionist at his office, where he could keep an eye on me."

"I see."

"Robert didn't have kids. I guess he just wanted to take care of me. But now my parents know about my dancing, because I had to tell them the whole story when I was arrested."

"Oh, sorry. So you didn't know Mia then?"

She shook her head. "I saw her a couple of times when I was a kid, but not for about five years. She didn't recognise me at all when she visited the office. But Robert – he'd been over quite a bit since their relationship went wrong. He stayed with us occasionally." She sighed. "My brother is golden boy. My parents are in Canada at the moment, as my sister-in-law has just had a little boy. I'm the disappointment, a uni-drop out, that's why I was tight for money. They're due home next week and are insisting I go back to Gloucestershire to live with them. I don't want to. They'll be lecturing me the whole time. But with no job, I can't afford my rent." She looked down at her hands.

I felt awful. If it wasn't for me telling the police, she could have gone back to Chesham's and nobody would have been the wiser.

"I need help here in the café. And I've got a spare room," I said, without thinking it through.

I KNOCKED ON CAROL'S FRONT DOOR, WITH A TIN IN hand containing a sticky toffee pudding, for our dessert. Lynn had kindly agreed to catsit Constance for me, who was too poorly for house visits.

The door opened and Carol took the tin from me. She placed it in the porch and gave me a huge hug. “I’m so pleased to see you, poppet.”

“Thanks for looking after me. I’m sorry for putting your whole family through such inconvenience.”

“Nonsense, you’re part of the family. And family needs to stick together.” She called out. “Henry, your Becky is here.”

I picked up the cake tin and followed Carol to the kitchen which was decorated in country style with sage green shaker units and wooden worktops. I turned as I heard H’s voice behind me.

“I just said to Rachael, I hope this evening isn’t going to be as eventful as the last time you came for supper.” He leaned against the door frame, smiling.

“You and me both.” I laughed.

“Now, Henry, don’t you be teasing her. Get our Becky a drink.”

I felt warm inside as I joined the extended family for a meal of cooked meats, salads and jacket potatoes as we discussed baby Victoria’s upcoming christening. There was no mention of murder or police for the entire evening.

The stars twinkled in the clear night, as H walked me along the prom. For the first time in weeks, I felt relaxed and happy.

“Bye then,” he said and kissed me on the cheek.

“I’m so sorry for what went on…for messing up the meal.”

"Maybe we can meet up again soon? For dinner?"

I nodded and smiled as I watched him walk back up the prom.

THE FOLLOWING DAY, DANNIE TURNED UP WITH TWO suitcases of belongings and made herself comfortable in one of the spare rooms I had made up for her. I seemed to be making a habit of taking in strays, firstly Constance and now Dannie.

I opened up the café doors with my new lodger beside me and Annie burst in waving the newspaper.

"Izzy's article has been released. You're front-page news again."

I grabbed the paper; Izzy had taken so many pictures of me, I was interested to see which one she'd used. "You are joking," I said.

The headline read: *Medium Solves Mystery of the Body in Branden Bay.* And slap bang on the front, was a picture of me, cuffed to H with green gunk smeared on my face looking like the princess from Shrek, with my robe opened revealing my swim suit.

It was that moment, that I heard Dannie laugh for the first time.

"Where on earth did that picture come from?" I asked.

"Some social media site," Annie said.

"Typical." I wondered whether H would be pleased about being splashed on the front page with himself handcuffed to the heroine who supposedly caught the killer and saved the day.

"It's a great action shot," said Annie. "There are better pics inside, including some of the café. You're going to be overrun with customers today."

And she was right, it was the last week for my old percolator because I'd ordered the new coffee machine and it would be arriving soon.

We were joined by Jeff, also holding a copy of The Gazette. He was beaming because he'd had a mention. When Lynn arrived to help out, she smiled at me with pride in her eyes. And my poor Constance lay in a fluffy bed I'd bought for her to convalesce in, within my sight.

At the end of the day, I held Constance as I looked across to the prom, to see a vision of a neat and handsome Robert. He saluted me. I felt a gentle fuzz of electricity in my hand as I waved back, watching his ghost fade into a beam of light.

I vowed that vision would be my last brush with the paranormal.

A NOTE FROM KELLY.

Thank you very much for reading The Body in Branden Bay. Why not try the next book when Becky agrees to investigate whether the cause of accidents on Branden Bay Pier, are due to a poltergeist.

To Becky's relief, she finds no paranormal activity.

However, following her visit, someone is found dead on the popular tourist attraction. Even worse, their ghost turns up on her doorstep. Becky has no choice but to search for the killer.

Can Becky find the murderer before they kill again?

Find out in *The Haunting of Branden Bay*

Reviews are really helpful to an author so please leave one if you have a few moments.

If you would like to join my mailing list and receive a free digital copy of my novella about Becky's grandma Constance, then please visit www.kellymasonbooks.com

ACKNOWLEDGMENTS

I'd like to thank my creative writing tutor Rosemary Dun, both inside the OU and out! You encouraged me to pursue novel writing and gave me so much information and guidance, I'm still reading the handouts! You are amazing. Thanks also goes to my brilliant mentors Alison Knight and Jenny Kane of Imagine Creative Writing and their Novel in a Year course, which gave me lots of help and kept me on track. And Alison is also my editor - thanks for all you do xx

Thanks to the inspirational friends I met through the Romantic Novelists' Association, and the Bristol writing community (I'm too scared to list everyone in case I miss someone off!) And to my Beta readers Cinnomen Matthews McGuigan and Michelle Armitage. Thanks to Helen Blenkinsop who is a guru on the 'hook' and amazon ads. And thanks to my best writing friends – Callie Hill, Claire O'Conner and Jenny Taylor, for also being beta readers of this and my wider writing (and Shell Rice Mortimer) and for their love and support and for sharing the journey with me, especially Callie who is always there to listen.

Thank you to my advance reader team who are

really supportive and there for me, even from the first book. And for the lovely emails I get from those on my mailing list.

Thanks to Tracey Hadfield who always has a ghost hunting story to scare me with.

Thanks to my sassy cats, even though they boss me about on a daily basis.

And finally, thanks to Gary for putting up with me tapping away at the keyboard 24/7.

Printed in Dunstable, United Kingdom

67319881R00129